THE HARDY BOYS

The House on the Cliff

Original publication:
United States, Applewood Books, 1927

By **FRANKLIN W. DIXON**

DEDICATION

To all the children of the world, I dedicate this book.

You are the future, and the world is yours to explore. Dream big and reach for the stars. Be curious, be brave, and be kind.

The Hardy Boys stories are about adventure and excitement, but they are also about friendship, family, and overcoming adversity. I hope that these stories will inspire you to be your best selves and to chase your dreams.

Never give up on your dreams, no matter how difficult they may seem. You are capable of anything you set your mind to.

So go out there and explore the world. Find your own adventures and create your own stories. And most importantly, have fun!

P.S. Don't forget to read a book every day!

CONTENTS

ACKNOWLEDGMENTS

I would like to express my sincere gratitude to the librarian who first showed me the Hardy Boys books as a young boy. I was eight years old at the time, and I was immediately hooked. I spent the next few years reading every Hardy Boys book I could get my hands on.

Those books sparked my love of reading and adventure. They taught me the importance of friendship, courage, and perseverance. They also showed me that anything is possible if you set your mind to it.

I am so grateful to the librarian who introduced me to the Hardy Boys. She changed my life forever.

Thank you.

CHAPTER I

THE HAUNTED HOUSE

Three powerful motorcycles sped along the shore road that leads from the city of Bayport, skirting Barmet Bay, on the Atlantic coast. It was a bright Saturday morning in June, and although the city sweltered in the heat, cool breezes blew in from the bay.

Two of the motorcycles carried an extra passenger. All the cyclists were boys of about fifteen and sixteen years of age and all five were students at the Bayport high school. They were enjoying their Saturday holiday by this outing, glad of the chance to get away from the torrid warmth of the city for a few hours.

When the foremost motorcycle reached a place where the shore road formed a junction with another highway leading to the north, the rider brought his machine to a stop and waited for the others to draw alongside. He was a tall, dark youth of sixteen, with a clever, good-natured face. His name was Frank Hardy.

"Where do we go from here?" he called out to the others.

The two remaining motorcycles came to a stop and the drivers mopped their brows while the two other boys dismounted, glad of the chance to stretch their legs. One of the cyclists, a boy of fifteen, fair, with light, curly hair, was Joe Hardy, a brother of Frank's, and the other lad was Chet Morton, a chum of the Hardy boys. The other youths were Jerry Gilroy and "Biff" Hooper, typical, healthy American lads of high school age.

"You're the leader," said Joe to his brother. "We'll follow you."

"I'd rather have it settled. We've started out without any particular place to go. There's not much fun just riding around the countryside."

"I don't much care where we go, as long as we keep on going," said Jerry. "We get a breeze as long as we're traveling, but the minute we stop I begin to sweat."

Chet Morton gazed along the shore road.

"I'll tell you what we can do," he said suddenly. "Let's go and visit the haunted house."

"Polucca's place?"

"Sure. We've never been out there."

"I've passed it," Frank said. "But I didn't go very close to the place, I'll tell you."

Jerry Gilroy, who was a newcomer to Bayport, looked puzzled.

"Where is Polucca's place?"

"You can see it from here. Look," said Chet, taking him by the arm and bringing him over to the side of the road. "See where the shore road dips, away out near the end of Barmet Bay. Do you see that cliff?"

"Yes. There's a stone house at the top."

"Well, that's Polucca's place."

"Who is Polucca?"

"Who *was* Polucca, you mean," interjected Frank. "He used to live there. But he was murdered."

"And that's why the place is supposed to be haunted?"

"Reason enough, isn't it?" said Biff Hooper. "I don't believe in ghosts, but I'll tell the world there are some funny stories going around about that house ever since Polucca was killed."

"He must have been a strange fellow, anyway," commented Jerry, "to build a house in such a place as that."

Indeed, the Polucca place had been built on an unusual site. High above the waters of the bay it stood, built close to the edge of a rocky and inhospitable cliff. It was some distance back from the road, and there was no other house within miles. The boys had traveled a little more than three miles since leaving Bayport, and the Polucca place was at least five miles away. It could hardly have been seen, had it not been for its prominent position on top of the cliff, silhouetted clearly against the sky.

"He *was* a strange fellow," Frank observed. "No one knew very much about him. He didn't welcome visitors. In fact, he always kept a couple of vicious dogs around the place, so nobody cared to hang around there if they weren't invited."

"He was a miser," came from Joe Hardy.

"He may have been. At least that was the theory. Everybody said Polucca had a lot of money, but after his death there wasn't a nickel found in the house."

"Felix Polucca always said he wouldn't trust the banks," put in Biff Hooper. "But if he had any money I don't know where he made it, for he didn't work at anything and he mighty seldom came into the city."

"Perhaps he inherited it," Jerry suggested.

"Maybe. He must have had money at some time, to build that house. It's a great, rambling stone place that must have cost thousands."

"Is anybody living there now?"

The others shook their heads. "No one has lived there since the murder and I don't think any one ever will," said Frank Hardy. "The house is too far out of the way, for one thing, and then—the stories that have been going around—"

"Well, I won't say I believe any place is haunted, but the Polucca place is certainly strange. There have been queer lights seen there at night. On stormy nights, particularly. And once a motorist had a breakdown near there, so he went up to the house for help. He didn't know anything about the history of the place. He got the scare of his life!"

"What happened?"

"He decided when he went into the front yard that the place was deserted, and he was just going to turn away when he saw an old man standing at one of the upper windows, looking at him. He called out, and the old man went away, and although the motorist hunted all through the house he didn't find any trace of the old chap. So he left that place as quickly as he could."

"I don't blame him," remarked Jerry. "But the house sounds interesting. I'm game to visit it."

"So am I!" declared the others.

"Lead on!" laughed Chet. "It'll be a brave ghost that will tackle the whole five of us."

Jerry clambered on behind Chet, and Biff mounted Joe's motorcycle. The machines roared, and the little cavalcade started on its way down the shore road toward the house on the cliff.

Instead of being an aimless trip, the outing had now assumed all the aspects of an adventure. With the exception of Jerry, the boys had all passed by the Polucca place at one time or another, but none had ever ventured off the main road to explore the deserted place.

The lane leading into the Polucca grounds, never kept in good repair even during the owner's lifetime, was now almost indiscernible and was overgrown with weeds and bushes. The house itself was hidden from the roadway by trees. Most people gave the place a wide berth, whether they believed in ghosts or not, for the stories that had been told of the rambling stone building since the murder of Felix Polucca two years before were sufficient to indicate that there had been strange happenings in the old house. Whether or not they were of supernatural origin was a matter of debate.

The murder of Felix Polucca had been particularly brutal. He was an old Italian, suspected, as Frank said, of being a miser. He was very eccentric in his ways and most people considered that he was not quite sound mentally.

Be that as it may, Bayport was shocked one morning to learn that the old man had been found dead in the kitchen of his house, his body riddled with bullets. The motive, apparently, was robbery, for although it was popularly believed that the old man possessed a great deal of money that he kept with him in the house, it was never found, in spite of the most diligent search.

This was the gloomy history of the place the Hardy boys and their chums were now about to visit and explore. To add to the atmosphere of excitement that had possessed them from the moment the old house was mentioned, as they drew closer to the cliff, the sun retired behind a cloud and the sky gradually became darker.

Frank glanced up. Although the sky had been bright and clear when the party left Bayport, clouds had gathered in the east and it was plain that a storm was gathering.

"Looks as if we'll have to go into the Polucca place whether we want to or not," he called out to the others. "It's going to rain."

In a little while they came to the lane that led to the haunted house. In spite of the fact that it was overgrown with weeds and bushes, the boys were able to drive down the faintly defined roadway until at last a rusty iron gate barred their progress.

Frank, who was in the lead, got off his machine and kicked the gate open, the rusty chains clanking dismally as they fell from the staples. Then the party went on into the grounds.

Under the lowering sky that heralded the approaching storm, the grounds of the Polucca place were far from inviting. Dank, tall grass grew beneath the unkempt trees, and thistles and weeds sprouted up in the very center of the roadway. A rising wind stirred among the branches of the trees and the waving grasses rustled mournfully.

"Creepy sort of a place," muttered Jerry.

"Wait till you see the house," Chet advised.

Not one of them could restrain a slight shiver of apprehension when at last they came in view of the old stone building. It was framed in a mass of trees, bushes, and weed that threatened to engulf it from all sides. Weeds obscured the front door. Bushes grew up level with the sills of the vacant downstairs windows. Trees on either side and beyond the house extended trailing branches down over the roof. A shutter hung by one hinge from an upstairs window, and banged with every passing gust of wind.

A deathlike silence hung over the old building. Under the black clouds that now filled the entire sky it was imbued with an atmosphere of gloom and terror.

"Come on!" said Frank. "Now that we're here we may as well go through the place."

"Haven't seen any ghosts yet," laughed Chet, with an effort at being light-hearted. But in spite of himself, his tone seemed forced.

They left the motorcycles beneath a tree and advanced toward the old stone building. The front door was almost off its hinges, and it swung creakingly open at Frank's touch.

Frank stepped boldly into the hallway. The interior of the house was veiled in gloom, for the rear windows were boarded up, but the lads could see that everything was deep in dust. A staircase was before them, leading to the upper stories of the building. To the left, was a closed door.

"This must be the parlor," said Frank, as he flung the door open.

The room was empty. A stone fireplace was at one side, and as the boys came into the room a rat scuttled out of the fireplace and raced across the floor, disappearing through a hole in the wall. The sound made every one jump, for the boys' nerves were at a tension on account of the forbidding atmosphere.

"Just a rat!" said Frank.

His voice had the effect of calming the others.

They stood hesitantly in the middle of the deserted parlor. Joe went over to the window and looked out, but the view from the front window of the Polucca place was so lonely and gruesome, in its aspect of tangled trees and weeds and undergrowth under the lowering darkness of the sky, that he came back.

"Where shall we go next?" said Chet.

"Nothing much to see around here," said Frank, disappointed. "It's just an ordinary, dirty, old, deserted house. Let's explore upstairs, anyway—"

At that moment there was a startling interruption.

A weird shriek, quavering as if with terror, rang out from the upper part of the haunted house!

CHAPTER II

THE STORM

That shriek was the most fearful and uncanny sound the boys had ever heard. There was a diabolical malignance about it, like the scream of some blood-thirsty animal, yet there was no mistaking the fact that it was uttered by a human being.

As the quavering notes died away, the bare walls of the old house flung back the echoes so that the shriek seemed to be repeated again and again, but on a smaller scale.

The boys stared at one another, aghast. For a moment they were dumbfounded. Then Jerry muttered:

"I'm getting out of here!" and with that, he started for the door.

"Me too!" declared Biff Hooper, and Chet Morton followed him as he rushed for the doorway.

"What's the big idea?" asked Frank, standing his ground. "Let's stay and find what this is all about."

9

Joe, seeing his brother remain where he was, made no move to follow the others, although it was plain that the weird shriek had unnerved him.

"You can stay," flung back Jerry. "I'm not. This place is haunted, and I don't mean maybe!"

The three boys hastened through the doorway out into the hall and lost no time in regaining the front yard. Frank and Joe Hardy listened to their retreating footsteps. Frank shrugged his shoulders.

"I guess it gave them a pretty bad scare," he said to his brother. "We may as well go with them."

"I guess so," replied Joe, greatly relieved. They were alone in the gloomy and deserted old house, and as they stepped into the hallway Joe cast a cautious glance up the stairway. But there was nothing to be seen. The upper floor was veiled in shadow. The house was in silence that seemed even heavier than before.

When the two Hardy boys got outside they found the others waiting for them in the shelter of some trees about a hundred yards from the house. The three were discussing the strange occurrence in excited tones, and when the Hardy boys came up to them Jerry said:

"I don't have to be convinced any further. The place is haunted, sure. No other way to explain it."

"There's not much sense in running away from a sound," remarked Frank lightly. "If we had seen something, it might be different. I don't believe in ghosts and I'd like to get to the bottom of this. It's foolish to run away. Let's go back."

Chet Morton and Biff Hooper looked a trifle ashamed of themselves because of their precipitous flight from the house while the Hardy boys had remained.

"I got the scare of my life," Chet confessed. "Just the same I'm game to go back if you want to."

"How about you, Biff?"

Biff Hooper scratched his head reflectively. "I'm none too anxious to go back in there again," he admitted. "Not that I'm scared, of course!" he added hastily. "But I don't see where we'd learn anything, anyway."

"Well, Joe and I are going back. That's settled," declared Frank. "We want to get to the bottom of this mystery."

"Mysteries are your meat!" observed Biff. "Well, when you come to think of it, this is a good chance for a little detective work."

He alluded to the fact that the Hardy boys were amateur detectives of some renown in Bayport. They came by their gift naturally, for their father, Fenton Hardy, had been for years on the detective staff of the New York police. Of late years he had been living in Bayport conducting a private detective service of his own with great success. He was known from one end of the country to the other as an exceptionally brilliant investigator.

Frank and Joe Hardy, his sons, were ambitious to follow in their father's footsteps, although their mother wished them to prepare themselves for medicine and the law respectively. But the lure of Fenton Hardy's calling was persistent, and the two boys were bent on proving to their parents that they were capable of becoming first-class detectives.

They had given proof of this already by helping their father in a small way on a number of cases, but their first big success had been achieved when they solved the mystery of a jewel and bond robbery from Tower Mansion in Bayport. The story of this has been related in the first and preceding volume of this series, "The Hardy Boys: The Tower Treasure," wherein was recounted how the Hardy boys solved the mystery of the robbery when the Bayport police and even Fenton Hardy himself were baffled.

"I'd rather tackle a good mystery than eat," laughed Frank.

"And here is one right to hand. Let's go back."

Biff Hooper did not care to seem guilty of cowardice by staying behind while his companions returned to the house and he was on the point of a reluctant consent when the matter was suddenly solved for them all by a downpour of rain.

Storm clouds had been gathering in the sky for the past hour and there had been dull rumblings of thunder. Now an uneasy wind stirred the branches of the trees and rustled dismally among the undergrowth. There was a spatter of raindrops, and then the storm broke in abrupt violence. Rain poured down in sheets.

"The motorcycles!" cried Frank.

Turning up their coat collars, the boys ran through the thick grass until they reached the place where their machines had been parked.

"I saw an old shed near the house," called out Joe. "We can put the bikes under cover."

There was an abandoned wagon shed near the rear of the house, and toward this refuge the lads trundled the heavy motorcycles. Although the shed was almost falling to pieces, the roof was still in fairly good condition and the machines were safe from the downpour.

"Come on," said Frank, when the motorcyles had been placed under cover. "Let's go back into the house."

He led the way, running across the open space from the shed, through the driving rain, and Joe followed. The others after a moment of hesitation, came after them.

The back door of the house was open and the lads ran up the steps into the shelter of the building. They were in a room that had evidently been used as a kitchen, and although rain came in slanting streaks through the open windows, the glass of which had long since been shattered, they were at least sheltered from the downpour that had assumed redoubled violence. The rain drummed on the roof of the old house and poured from black skies on the near-by wagon shed. Thunder rolled and rumbled threateningly, and every once in a while a sheet of lightning tore a band of lurid light across the gloom.

Chet took off his cap, which was drenched, and tried to dry it out. The others stood by the window, looking out at the terrific downpour.

Then came the second shriek!

It rang out suddenly, at a time when none of the lads was talking and it was a replica of the first—a quavering, long drawn out yell, that seemed to freeze the blood in their veins.

No sooner had it died away than there came a terrific clap of thunder, and then the rain seemed to beat down on the roof of the old house in a frenzy.

In the gloomy, dusty kitchen, the boys stared at one another.

Frank broke the silence.

"I'm going to find out about this!" he declared firmly, striding over to the door that led to the interior of the house.

"Me too," said Joe.

Taking heart by the Hardy boys' example, the others crowded at their heels.

Frank flung open the door and strode into the room beyond. It was a very gloomy chamber, for the one window was boarded up, but when their eyes became accustomed to the meager light the boys saw that a door on the far side of the room led into a hallway. It was evidently not the hallway that they had already been in at the front of the house, but presumably one that led to a side door.

"Nothing here," said Frank, "I'd like to find those stairs. That yell came from the upper part of the house."

The boys made their way across the room. Outside they could hear the sweep of the rain and the steady rumblings of the thunder, for the storm was now at its height. Through the chinks of the boards over the window they could occasionally see the lurid glare of lightning.

Suddenly there was a blast of wind that seemed to shake the entire house. A sharp, violent noise immediately behind them made every boy jump with surprise.

They wheeled about.

The door behind them had been blown shut. Biff Hooper, who was nearest, grasped the knob and tried to open it. He wrenched and tugged at the door, but it remained obstinate.

"We're locked in!" he muttered.

"We can get out, all right," said Frank. "There must be a door in this side hall."

He walked across the room and entered the hallway.

At the same instant a maniacal howl rang through the old house. The hollow echoes magnified its volume.

A flash of lightning illuminated the startled faces of the five boys. With one accord they rushed into the hallway. It was a narrow place, heavy with dust, and their feet thudded heavily on the mouldy flooring.

Crash!

At the far end of the hall they had a glimpse of falling plaster that fell in a great heap to the floor. A dense cloud of dust arose and filled the narrow chamber.

"Run for your lives!" yelled Frank.

But no sooner were the words out of his mouth than there came a ripping, crackling sound from overhead. Immediately above them, a large part of the ceiling, disturbed no doubt by the vibrations of their feet as they ran into the hall, had given

14

way. A wide crack that showed in the plaster quickly became wider, and then, with a terrific roar, half the hall ceiling came tumbling down upon the lads.

They were buried in dust and lathes and plaster that came upon them in such an avalanche that they were thrown to the floor. The splintering of wood and ominous crackling that followed, indicated that more of the ceiling was about to go, and then came a roar even louder than the first, as another avalanche of débris rolled down upon them.

Was the Polucca house falling in?

CHAPTER III

EMPTY TOOL BOXES

When he was knocked off his feet by the impact of falling débris, Frank Hardy crouched down, protecting his head as well as possible, until the downfall was over. Although a great deal of rubbish descended, it was not heavy material and when at last the rain of plaster and splintered lathes had ceased Frank knew that he was uninjured, although he was almost buried in the heap and half smothered by the thick dust that rose all about him.

He managed to get to his feet, fighting his way clear of the rubbish, and the first sight that met his eyes was an arm, sticking out of the débris near by. He seized the outstretched hand and dragged the owner to safety, discovering that it was his brother Joe.

By this time the others were beginning to extricate themselves, and within a few minutes all five boys, covered with dust from head to foot, had scrambled out to the clear floor in the middle of the hall. No one was injured, although Joe and Jerry complained of bruises about the head and shoulders.

"Let's get out of here!" exclaimed Chet, as soon as he could get his breath. "I'm not going to fool around this house any longer." He looked about him for some means of escape.

"I don't think it's very healthy myself," Frank agreed. He saw a door at the side of the hall and, going over, tried to open it.

But the door was locked fast, and although he kicked at it and shoved against the panels with all his strength he was unable to budge it.

"There's a window," declared Joe. "Let's break our way out."

The window was boarded over, but the glass was already shattered, so Chet and Jerry, picking up rocks that had tumbled down in the débris from the walls and ceiling, pounded at the boards.

"We'd better keep moving," advised Biff Hooper. "Perhaps the rest of the place will start caving in on us."

There was a splintering sound as one of the boards fell loose, revealing the rain-soaked trees and bushes outside. Another onslaught with the rocks and another board fell away, leaving a space sufficient to admit of the passage of a human body.

"Gee, that looks good to me!"

"Let's get out of here quick!"

"That suits me!"

"Don't lose any time—this whole building may be coming down!"

As the last words were uttered the boys heard another crash behind them. It was so close that it made all of them jump.

"Hurry up, everybody!" yelled Biff Hooper.

"Can't get out any too fast for me," returned Jerry.

"You said it!" muttered Chet.

One by one the boys scrambled up on the window sill and squeezed their way out between the boards until at last all were standing outside the old house. The storm was still raging. Rain poured down in a drenching torrent.

"Now let's get as far away from this place as we can travel!" said Jerry. "Somebody is going to get killed if we stick around here much longer."

He was pale with fright and it was plain that the strange experiences of the past hour had completely unnerved him.

"That's the way I feel about it," agreed Biff Hooper. "I'm not a bit comfortable around here. Let's beat it."

"I'd like to find out what is wrong with the place," persisted Frank doggedly.

"You couldn't drag me back in there with a team of horses," objected Chet. "Let's clear out. I've had enough of it."

"Come on," urged Jerry. "There's no use going back. The whole place will cave in on us if we aren't careful. And anyway, there's something fishy about the house."

Frank saw that the others were determined on leaving, in spite of the pouring rain, so, reluctantly, he gave in, and the five boys hastened around the side of the house over to the shed where they had left the motorcycles.

"We can at least stay in the shed until the rain goes over," he said.

"Not on your life," declared Chet Morton. "I'm going to put as much distance between little me and that haunted house as I can. That place gets on my nerves."

And with that he began tinkering with the machine preparatory to starting it.

Frank and Joe decided that no good would be served by arguing the matter, so they prepared to leave with the others although they privately resolved to return to the Polucca place at the earliest opportunity, to investigate the mystery of the house on the cliff more thoroughly.

Jerry and Biff Hooper took their places, and in a few minutes the three motorcycles drove slowly out of the shed and across the yard toward the lane.

It was then that they heard the laugh!

From the haunted house came a harsh, mocking laugh that rang out in peals of derisive merriment. It continued for several seconds, and could be heard quite plainly even above the noise of the engines and the drumming of the rain on the roof.

Then it stopped, abruptly.

The boys looked at one another.

"Did you hear some one laugh?" asked Frank, unable to believe his ears.

"You bet I did!" exclaimed Chet. "And that *does* settle it. I'm leaving here right away."

"That was the most nerve-racking laugh I ever heard in my life," declared Jerry. "Let's get out of here, quick."

"Somebody's playing a joke on us!" Frank said angrily. "I'm going back."

"Joke, nothing! That place is haunted. Come on."

And with a roar, Chet's motorcycle leaped forward as he headed down the lane toward the main road. Joe, after looking behind and motioning to his brother to stay with the party, followed him. Soon the three motorcycles were speeding down the lane.

And from the haunted house came peal after peal of that same demoniacal laughter, as though mocking their flight. Then, as they rode on through the streaming rain and the haunted house was lost to sight among the wet and sodden trees, the laughter died away.

When they reached the main road the boys turned their motorcycles in the direction of Bayport and for more than five minutes the machines rocked and swerved as they sped along through the muddy ruts. The boys were soaked to the skin and water dripped from the peaks of their caps into their eyes. The rain poured down with redoubled violence and the others could scarcely see Chet's machine through the misty downpour. Chet was making such good time back to Bayport that they found it difficult to keep up with him.

Frank Hardy was still dissatisfied. He had really wanted to remain behind and probe the mystery of the house on the cliff further. He held no stock in the ghost theory. The shrieks and the mocking laugh, he was sure, were of human origin. But what could have been the motive? It may have been that some boys had been in the house when they arrived and had simply seized the opportunity to play a joke on them.

"In that case," he muttered to himself, "the story will be all over the Bayport high school by Monday and we'll be kidded within an inch of our lives for running away. We should have stayed behind."

Something told him, however, that this was no ordinary schoolboy prank. The incident of the fallen ceiling had unnerved him slightly. It was only by good luck that none of them had been seriously hurt. Of course, it may have been entirely accidental, but it seemed to have happened at a strangely opportune time. Then the recollection of the shrieks and the mocking laugh came back to him again and he shivered as he recalled the maniacal intensity of the tones.

"If it was any fellow like ourselves he was a mighty good actor," Frank said to himself. "I've heard of a person's blood running cold, but I never knew what it meant until I heard those yells."

Suddenly his motorcycle began, as he termed it, "acting up." It coughed, lurched, back-fired explosively, and then the engine died.

"What a fine time for a breakdown," Frank said, as he dismounted.

Joe drew up alongside. "What's the matter?" he called.

"Engine broke down."

"Gosh, aren't you lucky!" exclaimed Joe, grinning. "There's a shed over at the side of the road. Bring it over under cover."

He pointed to a tumble-down shed near by. Frank realized that it might take some time to discover the trouble, so he trundled the motorcycle over to the refuge his brother had indicated. In the meantime, Chet Morton had looked back, to find that the others were not following him, and had decided to return. The roar of his machine could be heard through the rain as he rode back toward them.

In the shelter of the shed, Frank first of all took off his coat and cap, which were dripping wet, and hung them up on a projecting board. Then, as Joe and Jerry stood by, glad of the chance to get in out of the rain, he rolled up his sleeves and prepared to find the source of the trouble.

They could hear Chet calling for them, as he drove along the road in the rain.

"Thinks we're lost," laughed Joe. He went over to the front of the shed and hailed their companion. "Come on up here!" he shouted. "Had a breakdown."

Grumbling audibly, Chet dismounted and came over toward the shed.

In the meantime, Frank had opened the tool box of his motorcycle.

The others were startled by a sudden exclamation. Frank was staring at the tool box, with a bewildered expression on his face.

"My tools!" he exclaimed. "They're gone!"

The other boys crowded around. The tool box was empty.

"Did you have them when you left Bayport?" asked Joe.

"Of course I did. I never go anywhere without them. Who on earth could have taken them?"

"You can have mine," offered Joe, going over to his own motorcycle. He snapped open the tool box on his machine and then gave a shout of astonishment.

"Mine are gone too!"

CHAPTER IV

THE CHASE IN THE BAY

The boys stared at one another in bewilderment.

"I know my tool box was full when I left home," said Frank.

"And so was mine," came from Joe. "I was using the pliers just before we started out."

"Where could they have gone?"

"They must have been stolen while the motorcycles were in the shed at the Polucca place," Chet suggested.

"It's the only time they could have been taken," declared Frank. "It was the only time they were left unguarded."

Joe was frankly puzzled.

"But we didn't see any one around the place," said Jerry.

"No—but there was some one there. We heard those shrieks and the laugh. Some one stole those tools while we were in the house."

"It's some kind of a practical joke, that's what I'm beginning

23

to think," declared Frank. "Let's go back and get those tools."

"Not on your life," objected Jerry decisively. "This is a little too much. First of all we hear those shrieks, and then the house almost comes down around our ears, and now we find that the tools have been stolen by somebody we didn't see. We're safer away from there."

Biff Hooper nodded agreement.

"That's what I think. There's something queer about that house. We'll get into trouble if we go butting in any more."

"But we want our tools!"

"Good night!" Chet exclaimed. "Perhaps mine are gone too." He ran out of the shed over to the road and hastily examined the tool box on his machine. Then he straightened up with an audible sigh of relief.

"Thank goodness, they're here! Guess whoever took the others figured he had enough."

"I'm going back!" declared Frank.

"If you do, you'll have to excuse me," Chet said. "You're welcome to use my tools to fix up your machine, but I won't go back with you."

"Me neither," chimed in Jerry and Biff simultaneously.

Frank and Joe were silent. They wanted to go back to the Polucca place and investigate the matter further, but they did not want to break up the party, so they decided it would be better policy to remain with their companions.

"All right," Frank said. "Lend me a pair of pliers and I'll have this trouble fixed up in no time."

He went over to Chet's motorcycle and got the desired tools. Then he began to tinker with his machine. It was only a minor defect, and a few minutes' work sufficed to repair the damage. In the meantime it was apparent that the rain was letting up, and by the time the Hardy boys took their motorcycles out of the shed and regained the road, it had died away to a mere drizzle.

"This has been some holiday!" Chet muttered, as he mounted his machine again. "I'm going home. Jerry, you and Biff had better come up to our place for dinner. How about you and Joe, Frank?"

"Thanks just the same, but we couldn't. We promised to be back home this afternoon."

"There's a side road that turns off here that makes a nice short-cut to our farm. I guess I'll go that way. There should be room for three on this bike, with a little crowding."

Jerry and Biff Hooper clambered on the motorcycle with Chet Morton and started off. The Hardy boys followed on their own machines until they reached the side road, about a hundred yards away. There the others left them, after shouting good-bye. Frank and Joe watched Chet's motorcycle, heavily loaded, disappear into the mists that hovered over the road, and then they prepared to continue their journey back to Bayport.

The shore road dipped at that point and wound down along the edge of the bay in a deep spiral, which brought them at one point almost back to the cliff at the top of which the Polucca place was located, although by now they were nearer the water's edge. From there the road sloped directly down to the shore, then ran along the edge of the bay and in toward the city.

Frank looked up toward the top of the cliff that loomed high above them. They could not see the Polucca place from where they were, as it was on the high ground and almost masked by trees, but the mystery of the place still preyed on their minds.

"I'd like to go back there yet," said Frank suddenly. "That

affair of the tools has me guessing."

"Me too. But I think we'd better go on home. We can come back some other time and look for them."

"One minute I think it was only a practical joke of some kind. And the next minute I think it's something a whole lot deeper than that. There's something strange going on up there."

"There were sure a lot of strange things going on when we struck the place—that's certain. I can hear those shrieks yet."

"Well, I guess you're right, Joe. We may as well go on home. But I'd like to get to the bottom of it."

"Whoever stole those tools made quick work of it. We weren't in the house very long."

"It proves that it wasn't a ghost, anyway."

"I never did believe in the ghost theory. No, some human being took those tools. And he was watching us, too. He saw us put the bikes in the shed and he took the tools while we were in the house."

"Unless they were taken after we left the bikes under the trees in the first place."

"He wouldn't have had time. We only stepped into the front room and then we all came out after that first shriek. No, the tools were taken when the bikes were in the shed."

The boys rode on. The rain had ceased now, but the road was greasy and they had to call on all their skill to keep from skidding as they drove down the steep road toward the bay, so they did not talk again until they reached the more level highway at the shore.

A sound out in the bay attracted Frank's attention and he looked out over the rolling sweep of waters. He could see a powerful motorboat plunging through the waves about a quarter of a mile out. It was just coming into view around the base of the cliff, and as Frank looked he saw the nose of still another boat emerging into sight. Each craft was traveling at high speed.

"Looks like a race!" remarked Joe.

The Hardy boys stopped their motorcycles and watched the two boats. But it was soon apparent that this was no friendly speed contest. The boat in the lead was zigzagging in a peculiar manner, and the pursuing craft was rapidly overhauling it. The staccato roar of the powerful boats was borne to the lads' ears by the wind.

"See! The other boat is chasing it!" Frank exclaimed. He had caught sight of the figures of two men standing in the bow of the pursuing craft. They were waving their arms frantically.

The first boat turned as though it were about to head inshore at the cliff and then, apparently, the helmsman changed his mind, for at once the nose of the boat pointed out into the open bay again. But the moment of hesitation had given the pursuers the chance they wanted, and swiftly the gap between the racing craft grew smaller and smaller.

The Hardy boys saw that there was but one man in the foremost craft. He was bent over the wheel. In the other boat they caught sight of one figure who had snatched up an object that appeared to be a rifle. To their amazement they saw him aim at the man in the leading craft. Then, across the water, they heard the sharp report.

The lone figure in the first boat dropped out of sight. Whether he had been hit or not the boys could not tell. But the craft did not slacken speed. Instead, it still continued to race madly through the waves.

But the pursuers rapidly drew closer until at last the boats were running side by side. They were so close together that it appeared as if a collision were imminent.

"The whole crowd of them will be killed if they aren't

careful!" muttered Frank.

Then, just when it seemed that both boats must crash together, the pursuing craft, as though it had given up the chase, veered abruptly away and headed out toward the middle of the bay.

The speed of the other boat decreased. The roar of its exhaust became intermittent.

"Engine trouble!" suggested Joe.

But there was more than engine trouble.

With startling violence, a sheet of flame leaped high into the air from the motorboat. There was a stunning explosion and a dense puff of smoke. Bits of wreckage were thrown high into the air, and in the midst of it all the Hardy boys, horrified, saw the figure of the man they had noticed before, as he was hurled into the water.

The whole boat was swiftly ablaze. Hardly had the wreckage begun to fall back into the water with spasmodic patterings and splashes than the craft was in flames from bow to stern.

"Look!" shouted Frank. "He's still alive!"

The man of the boat had been killed by neither the rifle shot nor the explosion.

They could see him struggling in the water not far from the blazing craft. His head was a dark oval above the water and he was slowly trying to swim ashore.

"He'll never make it!" gasped Joe.

"We'll have to try to save him!" answered his brother.

CHAPTER V

THE RESCUE

The Hardy boys knew that they had no time to lose.

It was evident from the struggles of the man in the water that he was not an expert swimmer. So far, he had not seen the boys, but they could hear him shouting for help, possibly thinking, however, that it was in vain, for it was a lonely part of the bay and the nearest farmhouse, outside of the deserted Polucca place, was more than half a mile down the road.

"Quick!" shouted Frank. "I see a rowboat up on the shore."

His sharp eyes had discerned a small boat almost hidden in a little cove some distance away at the bottom of a steep declivity that was the beginning of the cliff. It could not be reached by going along the shore, and the boys saw that they would have to go along the high ground and then descend to it, for a huge rock that jutted out of the deep water cut the cove off from the more open part of the beach.

They left their motorcycles on the side of the road and hurried back up the slope, then cut down across a narrow strip of weeds and grass until they came to the top of the declivity. They could still see the victim of the explosion struggling in the waves. The man had seized a piece of wreckage and was able to remain afloat, but the boys knew it was only a matter of time before his strength would give out.

"Looks to be almost all in," remarked Frank.

"I wonder if he's anybody we know," came from his brother.

"It isn't likely." Frank reached out suddenly and caught hold of Joe's arm. "Look out there or you may break a leg."

"It certainly is mighty slippery," answered Joe, as he managed to regain his footing. He had come close to going heels over head on the rocks.

Slipping and scrambling, they made their way down the slope toward the little cove. Rocks went rolling and tumbling ahead of them. The distance was only a few yards, but the slope was steep and a false step might result in broken bones.

But they reached the bottom in safety and there they came upon the rowboat. It was battered and old, but evidently still seaworthy.

"Into the water with her!" said Frank.

They seized the boat and the keel grated on the shingle as the little craft was launched. Swiftly, they fixed the oars in the locks and then they scrambled into their places.

They began to row with strong, steady strokes out toward the man in the bay. He had seen them, and was now shouting to them to hurry.

"He'd be better off if he kept quiet," Joe said. "He's only wasting his strength."

Evidently this thought occurred to the victim of the wreck or else he was becoming weaker, for his cries died away and the boys did not hear him again.

Frank thought he may have gone beneath the waves, and he cast a quick look around. But the fellow was still in view, clinging desperately to his bit of wreckage.

The motorboat in the background was still blazing fiercely. Flames were shooting high in the air and the craft was plainly doomed. A great pillar of smoke was rolling into the sky from the burning boat.

As for the other motorboat, Frank could hear the roar of its exhaust as it continued its flight out into the bay. For a while he could see its dim shape, when he turned around once in a while, but then the fleeing boat disappeared into the mist and the gloom.

The boys exerted all their strength and the little rowboat fairly leaped over the waves. Both were good oarsmen and it was not long before they had drawn close to the man in the water.

But it looked as though they would be too late.

When they were only a few yards away Frank looked around, to shout encouragement to the victim of the wreck. Even as he looked, he saw the man wearily give up his grasp on the piece of wreckage to which he had been clinging. Frank had a glimpse of the white face and the despairing eyes and then the man sank slowly beneath the waves.

"He's drowning, Joe!" shouted Frank, as he bent to his oar again.

With a mighty effort they brought the boat close by the place where the man had gone down.

Frank leaped to the side of the boat and peered down into the depths. He began taking off his coat, preparatory to diving to the rescue.

Then the fellow came to the surface again, gasping for breath, but so weak that he could scarcely make a struggle. He emerged from the water, right beside the boat and Frank leaned over, grasping him by the hair. This sufficed to prevent the man from sinking for the second time, and Frank managed to get a grip on the collar of his coat.

Then, with Joe helping and in imminent danger of upsetting the boat, he managed to drag the stranger to the side of the craft.

The fellow was a dead weight, for he had lapsed into unconsciousness when Frank seized him, but somehow they contrived to get him into the boat, and there he lay, sprawled helplessly, more dead than alive.

"We'd better get him to shelter some place and revive him," said Joe. "We can't do much for him here."

"How about that farmhouse down the bay?"

"The very place. Where is it?"

They finally located the farmhouse, a snug little building back off the main road some distance down the bay. It meant considerable rowing, but there was a life at stake.

The blazing motorboat near by was a roaring mass of flames. Then it began to sink beneath the waves. There was a great hissing sound and a heavy cloud of steam as the craft sank lower and lower into the water, its blazing embers blackening to the touch of the sea. Swiftly, at last, the boat disappeared. Its stern seemed to hesitate for a moment, and then it slid quickly down into the waves and the only trace was a widening pool of oil and scattered wreckage on the surface of the water.

But the Hardy boys were too busy to give more than passing notice to the spectacle. Their immediate problem was to get the stranger under shelter.

Frank decided that there was no necessity for first aid. The man had been conscious when he rose from the water the first time, so there could not be much water in his lungs. He had simply given in to exhaustion and fatigue resulting from his long struggle in the waves.

They headed the boat down the bay, in a direct line with the little farmhouse, which they could see nestling among the trees. They had already spent much energy in rowing out to the rescue of the stranger, but they fell to the new task with a will. Rowing with machine-like precision, they felt the little boat respond to every effort, and it fairly leaped along. This time they had the wind and the waves with them and they made good time.

The man they had rescued lay face downward in the bottom of the boat. He was a slim, black-haired fellow. His clothes, which of course were soaked with water, were cheap and worn, the sleeves being frayed at the cuffs. They could not see his face, but they judged him to be young. He was still unconscious.

Frank let Joe take his oar for a moment, and crouched down beside the stranger. He turned the man over and the limp form lolled about as helplessly as a bag of salt. As they had surmised, he was a young fellow, with sharp, clean-cut features. He wore a cheap shirt, open at the throat.

Frank pressed his ear to the fellow's chest and listened for signs of life. Finally he straightened up, with a mutter of satisfaction.

"His heart's beating all right," he told Joe. "He's alive, at any rate. Just all in. He'll come to after a while."

He returned to his oar and the little boat skimmed over the waves on toward the farmhouse in the distance.

The boys rowed until the muscles of their arms were aching, but at last they drew near the shore and finally the pebbles grated underneath the keel. Frank leaped out and dragged the boat part way up on the beach. Then, between them, they carried the unconscious man up the rocky shore toward the farmhouse.

They found a path that led through a field up to the back door of the house, and although their burden was heavy they managed to carry the still figure, limp and motionless, across the field.

A gaunt, kindly-faced woman came hurrying out of the house at their approach, and from the orchard near by came a man in overalls. The farmer and his wife had seen them.

"Laws! what's happened now?" asked the woman, wide-eyed, as they came up to her.

"This man was mighty nearly drowned out in the bay," explained Frank. "We saw your house—"

"Bring him in," boomed the farmer. "Bring him indoors."

The woman ran ahead of them and held the door open. With the farmer giving aid, the boys carried the unconscious man into the house and placed him on a couch in the comfortably furnished living room. The farmer's wife glanced dubiously at the stream of water that dripped from the victim's clothes, for she was a tidy soul and she had just scrubbed the floor that morning, but her better nature overcame her housewifely instincts and she hastened out to the kitchen to prepare a hot drink.

"Best rub his hands," suggested the farmer. He was a burly man with a black beard. "It'll bring the blood back to his cheeks. One of you take off his boots and we'll wrap his feet up in warm flannels."

For the next five minutes the house was a scene of excitement as the farmer and his wife bustled about and the Hardy boys rubbed industriously at the hands and feet of the unconscious man, trying to restore him to consciousness. At last there was a sign of reviving life.

The man on the couch stirred feebly. His eyelids fluttered. His lips moved, but no words came. Then the eyes opened and the man stared at them, as though in a daze.

"Where am I?" he muttered faintly.

"You're safe," Frank assured him. "You're with friends."

"Pretty—near—cashed in—didn't I?"

"Yes, you pretty nearly drowned. But you're all right now."

"It was Snackley!" said the stranger, as though talking to himself. "Snackley got me—the rat!"

CHAPTER VI

SNACKLEY

At that moment the farmer's wife appeared, bringing a drink of hot ginger and water, which the man on the couch gulped down gratefully.

"We'll put him in the spare room, Mabel," decided the farmer. "He needs a good warm bed more'n anything else just now. I'll look after him, if these boys here will help me."

"I—I think I was shot—" muttered the stranger. He motioned weakly toward his side.

Frank leaned over.

"Why, there's blood on his coat!" he exclaimed.

A hasty examination showed that the stranger was right. There was a bullet wound in his right side. It was evidently not serious, merely a flesh wound, but it had bled freely and the man was weakened.

Gently, the boys helped removed his clothing, and with warm water and a sponge the farmer bathed the wound. The bullet had passed right through the fellow's coat after searing a path across his side. Disinfectant was then applied, the stranger gritting his teeth with pain, and after that the bandages were put in place.

"Now we can put him to bed. Can you walk, stranger?"

The man made an effort to rise, and then fell back weakly upon the couch.

"I'm afraid—I can't!"

"All right, then, we'll carry you. Give me a hand with him, lads."

Between them, they carried the wounded man upstairs into a plain but comfortably furnished room. Here he was put to bed and covered with warm blankets. With a sigh of relief, he closed his eyes.

"He's weak from loss of blood. That's mostly what's the matter with him," the farmer said. "We'll let him have a good sleep."

They left the room, and when they went out into the kitchen again the Hardy boys told the farmer and his wife of the strange adventure they had just been through. The farmer listened thoughtfully.

"Queer!" he observed. "Mighty queer!" Then, glancing significantly at his wife, he said: "What d'you think of it, Mabel?"

"I think the same as you, Bill, and you know it. Most like it's been another of them smuggling mix-ups."

The farmer nodded. "I've an idea it's somethin' like that."

"Smuggling!" exclaimed Frank.

"Sure! There's quite a bit of smuggling goes on around Barmet Bay, you know. Leastways, there has been in the past few months. That's been *my* suspicions, anyway. I've seen too many motorboats out in the bay of late, and I've heard too many of 'em prowlin' around at night. If it's not smugglin' it's some other kind of unlawful business."

"Do you think this fellow may have been shot in some kind of a smugglers' quarrel?"

The farmer shrugged. "Maybe. Maybe. I ain't sayin' nothin'. It ain't safe to say anythin' when you don't know for certain. But I wouldn't be a mite surprised."

Mr. and Mrs. Kane, as they introduced themselves, were just about to have dinner, and they invited the Hardy boys to stay. This the lads were glad to do, as they were very tired by their exertions of the morning, and were already feeling the pangs of hunger.

They sat down to the simple but ample meal, typical farm fare of roast beef and baked pork and beans, with creamy mashed potatoes, topped off with a rich lemon pie, frothy with meringue, and fragrant coffee. During the meal they discussed the strange affair of the bay. The Hardy boys did not mention their experiences at the Polucca place, for they had learned that one of the chief requisites of a good detective is to keep his ears open and his mouth shut and to hear more than he tells. At that, one mystery was enough for one dinner.

"I'd like to find out more about this affair," said Frank, when the meal was concluded and Mr. Kane sat back luxuriously in his chair and puffed at his pipe. "Perhaps that fellow is awake now."

"Wouldn't do any harm to see. You might ask him some questions. I'm just as curious about it as you are yourself."

They went upstairs. The stranger was sleeping when they looked into the room, but the slight noise they made awakened him and he gazed at them dully.

"Feeling better?" Joe asked.

"Oh, yes," replied the stranger weakly. "I must have lost a lot of blood, though."

"That was when they shot at you just before the boat blew up," said Frank.

The man in the bed nodded, but said nothing.

"What's your name, stranger?" asked Mr. Kane bluntly.

The man in the bed hesitated a moment.

"Jones," he said, at last.

It was so evidently a false name that the Hardy boys glanced at one another, and the farmer scratched his chin doubtfully.

"How come you to be in such a mess as this?" he asked, at last. "What were they shootin' at you for?"

"Don't ask me, please," said the mysterious Jones. "I can't tell you. I can't tell you anything."

"I suppose you know these young fellers saved your life?"

"Yes—I know—and I'm very grateful. But don't ask me any questions. I can't tell you anything about it."

"You won't even tell them? Not after they saved your life?"

Jones shook his head stubbornly.

"I can't explain anything about it. Please go away. Let me sleep."

Frank and Joe signaled to the farmer that it would be best if they withdrew, so they left the room and closed the door. When they went back downstairs the farmer was grumbling to himself.

"I'm hanged if he ain't the most close-mouthed lad I've ever seen!" he declared. "You saved his life and he won't tell you why he come to be racin' around the bay in a motorboat with fellows shootin' at him."

"He must have some good reason. It's his own business, after all," reflected Frank. "We can't force him to explain anything."

"He's in with them smugglers, that's what he is!" declared Mr. Kane, with conviction.

"I guess we had better be getting back home. Do you mind keeping him here? We can have him moved to a hospital."

The farmer shook his head.

"Smuggler or not, he stays here until he gets better. Nobody ever said Bill Kane turned a sick man out of doors, and nobody ever will. He stays here until he gets better."

"We'll come back in a day or so and see how he is getting along," Joe promised.

"He'll have the best of care here. Whether it's smugglin' or not that he's been mixed up in, it doesn't matter. My wife and I will look after him."

The Hardy boys arranged to have the rowboat returned to its mooring place, then took their leave of the good-hearted farmer and his wife and made their way out to the road. Then they went back to the place where they had left their motorcycles, and in a short while were speeding again on their return to Bayport.

"That fellow is certainly a queer stick," remarked Joe, as he and his brother motored toward home.

"I'll say he is!" answered Frank. "There's something mighty queer about all this, and don't you forget it!"

It was mid-afternoon when they turned their motorcycles into the driveway beside the Hardy home, and after they had put the machines in the garage they went into the house. They found their father, Fenton Hardy, in his den just off the library. He was never too busy to talk to his sons, and when they came in he put down the papers he was studying and leaned back in his chair.

"Well, what have you two been up to to-day?" he inquired, smiling.

"We've had a real adventure, this time, dad," Frank told him. "We were out to the old Polucca place with some of the fellows."

"That's the haunted house, isn't it? See any ghosts?"

The boys looked at one another. "No, we didn't see any ghosts, exactly," said Joe. "But—"

"You don't mean to tell me you heard some!" Fenton Hardy threw back his head and laughed with delight.

"You may laugh; but some mighty queer things happened out there," insisted Joe.

Whereupon the brothers told their father of the strange experiences at the deserted farmhouse. But Mr. Hardy refused to take them seriously.

"Some of your school chums playing a joke on you," he said, dismissing the affair. "They'll be laughing their heads off about it right now."

"But how do you account for the tool boxes being robbed?"

"They just did that to make it a little more mysterious. Probably they will hand you back your tools at school on Monday, just to prove their story."

This aspect of the situation had not occurred to the boys. They began to look a bit sheepish. If it had been the work of practical jokers it was only natural that they would seek something definite whereby to prove the fact that they had been at the farmhouse.

"Gosh, we'll never hear the end of it, if that's the case," sighed Joe. "Oh, well, we'll just have to take it in good part. But we didn't tell you about what happened on the way

41

home. Tell him about it, Frank."

"Another adventure?"

"A real one. No practical joke about this."

Frank thereupon told their father about the two motorboats in Barmet Bay, about the chase and the resulting explosion. He modestly underestimated their own part in the rescue of the victim of the wreck, but Fenton Hardy nodded his head in satisfaction as the story went on.

"Good work! Good work!" he muttered. "You saved the fellow's life, anyway. And it looks as though you've stumbled on a mysterious bit of business in that motorboat chase. What did the man say his name was?"

"Jones," answered Frank doubtfully.

Fenton Hardy raised his eyebrows. "Of course—there are lots of Joneses in the world. It *might* be his real name. But more than likely it isn't. Would he tell you anything about the reason for the chase? Did you question him?"

"He wouldn't tell us anything at all. We made a few inquiries but he said he couldn't explain."

"Still more mysterious," reflected the detective. "Do you think he will talk when he gets better?"

"I'm afraid not. He seemed quite determined not to tell us anything about himself or about the men who were chasing him."

"Don't you remember, Frank?" exclaimed Joe. "When we brought him into the house, just as he became conscious again. What was it he said?"

"Oh, yes! I had forgotten. He said, 'Snackley got me, the rat.' Whatever that meant."

"Snackley!" exclaimed Fenton Hardy, starting up. "Are you sure he said Snackley? Are you sure that was the name?"

"I'm certain. Aren't you, Joe?"

"Yes, that was the name, all right."

"Well that *does* give us something to work on," the detective said. "Probably you have never heard of Snackley, but I have."

"Who is he?" asked Frank.

"Ganny Snackley is a noted criminal. He is a smuggler—one of the leaders of a ring of smugglers who bring in opium and other drugs from the Orient. Is it possible that he is bringing drugs into the country at Barmet Bay?"

CHAPTER VII

BOUND AND GAGGED

The Hardy boys were astonished by this information. Their father, tapping a pencil quickly on the desk, leaned forward in his chair.

"You may have stumbled on some information of great value," he said to them quietly. "I need hardly tell you that it is best to keep it to yourself. If Ganny Snackley is operating in this vicinity it will be a great feather in our cap to catch him."

"It's an unusual name," remarked Frank. "I'll bet that's the Snackley our man meant, all right."

"And the farmer said there was smuggling going on in the Bay," Joe pointed out.

"Of course, there always has been more or less smuggling carried on in Barmet Bay. But it's been on a small scale. Ganny Snackley and his gang are international smugglers. The last I heard of him he was operating up on the New England coast. But probably things grew too hot for him and he moved down here. He seems to have dropped completely out of sight for the past six months or so."

"Perhaps this man Jones, at the farmhouse, will talk later on."

"I'm going out there to interview him," said Fenton Hardy. "I'll wait a few days until he is feeling better. Of course the matter is one for the United States authorities, and as I haven't been assigned to the case I can't do very much. But perhaps I'll get some information I can use at some other time."

"Joe and I will go out to-morrow and see how he is getting along."

"Do so. But don't ask any questions. Don't let him think you are suspicious of him. Otherwise he'll be liable to sneak away as soon as he can, and we'll lose him altogether. He is under an obligation to you now because you saved his life, so it will seem quite natural for you to come back to see him. If you think he is recovering quickly, let me know and I'll go out right away and talk to him. If you think he will be there for several days yet, we'll just let him stay until he feels better."

"Perhaps he is a detective himself," Frank suggested.

"That had occurred to me," admitted Mr. Hardy. "If that's the case, I'll keep out of the affair. It's just probable that he is a Secret Service man who discovered Snackley's hang-out and was shot for his pains. That would explain why he wouldn't tell you anything about himself. But there's always the possibility that he is one of Snackley's enemies; and in that case I may be able to persuade him to talk."

Fenton Hardy asked the boys more questions about their adventure, but beyond a few trivial details they were unable to throw any further light on the mystery. However, it was decided that they should go back to the Kane farmhouse on the following day, which was Sunday, and report on the condition of the mysterious Mr. Jones.

With that they left their father, spending the rest of the afternoon in eager discussion and speculation concerning the strange events of the day. It had been an eventful holiday for them, and although they went over the incidents time and again they were unable to arrive at any solution of the puzzling affair in Barmet Bay. As for the happenings at the house on the cliff, they were inclined to accept their father's theory that some practical joker had been to blame.

Next morning, after church, they took the motorcycles out of the garage and prepared to ride out to the Kane farmhouse, there to make inquiry as to the condition of the man they had rescued on the previous day.

"Remember!" warned their father. "Don't ask him too many questions or he'll get suspicious. Just find out how long he is likely to remain at the farm. If his injuries aren't very serious he'll be leaving in a day or so and we want to check up on him."

The boys promised to follow the detective's instructions. Unlike the day previous, this Sunday was clear and bright, and the rain of the afternoon before had laid the dust so that they enjoyed their journey out along the shore road.

"It would be a bad joke on us if Mr. Jones left before we got there," remarked Joe.

"I don't think he will. That wound in his side was enough to keep him laid up for a few days. And, anyway, he lost so much blood yesterday that it would take him a while to get back his strength."

"I hope he isn't a detective."

"Why?"

"It would be great if we could get a chance to do some work on this case ourselves. If Ganny Snackley is in this neighborhood and the government detectives don't know of it, we would help dad land him."

"It *would* be a great chance," admitted Frank. "But I think we'll find our friend Jones is a detective. That is, if we ever find out anything definite about him. Why else should Snackley and his men try to kill him? For there's no doubt they left him for dead."

"Perhaps he was another smuggler that they wanted to get rid of."

"Maybe. But I think it's most likely he is a Secret Service man."

At length they arrived at the lane leading from the main road to the farmhouse. As their motorcycles roared down the drive they watched for some sign of life about the place. But there was no one in the orchard or in the barnyard. No one came out of the house. The place appeared to be deserted and, although it was a warm day, the doors were closed.

"This is queer," remarked Frank, as they brought their motorcycles to a stop and left them in the shade of a large tree near the back of the house, "Mr. and Mrs. Kane couldn't have gone away and left Jones there alone, could they?"

The boys went up to the door and rapped.

There was no answer.

"Try the front door," Joe suggested.

After a number of futile efforts, they went to the front door of the farmhouse. But here, although they banged on the panels, there was likewise no response.

"They must have gone out," said Joe.

"But what about Jones? They wouldn't leave him here alone. I can't understand this."

They went to the back door and rapped again and again. Still there was no answer. Frank tried the doorknob and found that the door swung open.

47

"They didn't lock the place up, anyway," he said. "Let's go in. If Jones is upstairs we'll go up and see him. Mr. Kane won't mind. Probably they didn't expect callers to-day."

They went into the kitchen and here they were surprised by the scene of disorder that greeted their gaze. The previous day they had been impressed by the neatness of the room, for Mrs. Kane was evidently the soul of tidiness. Now the kitchen looked as though an earthquake had shaken it.

Pots and pans were strewn about the floor. The table had been overturned. A chair lay upside down in a corner. A few cups and saucers lay in shattered bits beside the stove. The wood-box had been upset and the wood was scattered about. One window curtain had been partly torn from its fastenings.

"What on earth has happened here!" Frank exclaimed, in profound astonishment.

"Looks as if a cyclone came through."

"There's something queer about this! There's been a fight or a struggle of some kind here. Let's see what the rest of the house looks like."

The Hardy boys rushed into the next room. There an unexpected sight met their eyes.

Mr. and Mrs. Kane were seated in chairs in the middle of the room. They were unable to move, unable to speak, scarcely able to make a struggle.

The farmer and his wife were bound and gagged, tied to their chairs!

CHAPTER VIII

THE STOLEN WITNESS

Swiftly, the Hardy boys rushed over to Mr. and Mrs. Kane and began to release them. The farmer and his wife had been trussed up by strong ropes and they had been so well gagged that they had been unable to utter a sound. It was only a matter of a few minutes, however, before their bonds were loosened and the gags removed.

"Thank goodness!" exclaimed Mrs. Kane, with a sigh of relief, as the gag was taken away. Her husband, spluttering with rage, rose from his chair and hurled the ropes to one side.

"What happened?" asked the boys, in amazement.

For a moment Mr. and Mrs. Kane were unable to give a coherent account of their experience, owing to the strain they had undergone, but at last the farmer stumbled over to the window and pointed down the shore road.

"They went that way!" he roared. "That way! Follow them!"

"Who?"

"The rascals that tied us up. They took Jones away with them."

"Kidnapped him?"

"Yes—kidnapped him! There were four of them. They broke in here and tied up my wife and me. Then they went upstairs and carried Jones away with them. They dumped him into an automobile and made a getaway."

"Four men!"

"Four of the ugliest looking scoundrels you ever laid eyes on."

"How long ago?" asked Frank quickly.

"They didn't leave ten minutes ago. If you had been here just a few minutes earlier you would have met the whole crowd of them." The farmer was angry and excited. "But there's time yet. You can catch 'em. They went down the shore road."

"Come on, Joe!" shouted Frank. "Let's chase them. They've kidnapped Jones."

Joe needed no urging. The Hardy boys left the farmer and his wife rubbing their chafed wrists and ankles and hastened out of the house over to their motorcycles. Within a few seconds the staccato roar of the powerful machines broke out on the still air, and then they went rocking and swaying down the lane out on to the shore road.

"Some high-handed proceeding, I'll say," yelled Frank, to make himself heard above the roaring of the motorcycles.

"Those rascals ought to be in prison," returned his brother.

The boys followed in the direction the farmer had indicated. Frank then recollected that just before they had turned in toward the Kane farm he had seen a cloud of dust down the main road, evidently caused by a speeding automobile, but he had thought nothing of it at the time, for traffic along the shore highway occasioned no comment, especially on Sunday.

"If we had only been a little earlier!" he groaned.

"We'll catch up to them. They haven't much of a start. Maybe we can follow them to some town and have the whole gang arrested."

The motorcycles roared along at top speed. Both the Hardy boys were skilful drivers, and for a while Frank was able to follow the course of the car they were pursuing by watching the fresh tread mark in the dust. But when the road came to the place where it intersected with the road leading up to the Morton farm the tread mark became lost, as evidently another car had turned out of the side road in the meantime and obliterated the fresh tread here and there.

They passed the lane that led into the Polucca place and continued on down the shore road until they came to a hilltop that commanded a view of a wide stretch of country. Here they could see the road winding and dipping for a distance of more than a mile, until it was lost to sight in a grove of trees. But there was no sign of the automobile they were seeking.

"They've given us the slip, I guess," said Frank, as he brought his motorcycle to a stop.

"They had a good start and they weren't letting the grass grow under their feet, either. Think we should keep on?"

"There's not much use. We'd better go back to the farmhouse and hear what Mr. and Mrs. Kane have to say about this."

They turned their motorcycles about and headed back toward the farm. On the way they discussed the mysterious kidnapping.

"Evidently those men in the other motorboat saw us rescue Jones, or else they heard that he had been taken to the farmhouse," remarked Joe. "They must be desperate characters."

"I wonder what will happen to poor Jones now," said Frank gravely. "They tried to kill him in the first place. This time—"

"Do you think they'll murder him?"

"It looks like that. They didn't show him any mercy out in the bay. They left him for dead that time. Now they'll make sure of it."

Joe shuddered. "If they were going to kill him they'd hardly go to all that bother of kidnapping him," he pointed out. "Perhaps they just want to keep him out of the way. Perhaps they were afraid he would tell about their chasing him and setting fire to his motorboat."

"They were mighty anxious to get their hands on him, when they would come to the house in broad daylight and tie up Mr. and Mrs. Kane. Gee, it's lucky we came along when we did! They might have been left there for hours without being able to get loose."

When they got back to the farmhouse they found that the farmer and his wife had somewhat recovered from their harrowing experience, although they were still unnerved. Mrs. Kane, ever the true housewife, was already beginning to tidy up the kitchen and living room, for the intruders had upset everything in the struggle.

"We lost them," said Frank.

Kane nodded.

"I didn't think you'd catch them," he said. "They left here in too much of a hurry. But I hoped you would. They had a big high-powered car and they didn't waste any time getting away."

"There were four of them, you said?"

"Four. Ugly villains."

52

"What did they look like?"

"I didn't get much of a chance to see. It all happened too quick. One of them came to the door—he was a tall chap with a thin face—and asked if I was looking after a man who was almost drowned yesterday. I said that I was, so he told me he had come to take him away, that he was a brother of the fellow. I got kind of suspicious, and asked him his name. But in the meantime I had stepped outside the door, and before I knew it, some one jumped at me from behind. I put up a fight as best as I could, but the others came at me from around the corner of the house where they had been hidin' and before I knew it I was tied up. Then they tied up my wife and left us in the livin' room while they went upstairs."

"Did Jones put up a fight when they took him away?"

"He tried to. He hollered for help, but of course I couldn't do nothin' and he was too weak to fight much himself. They carried him downstairs and put him in the automobile. Then they drove away."

"There must be more to this affair than we imagine," reflected Frank. "It's getting serious when they break into a private home like this."

"You bet it's gettin' serious!" exclaimed the farmer. "It'll be mighty serious for them if they try it again." He motioned to the table where a shotgun was lying. "I've got that gun loaded and waitin' for the next gang that tries anything like that. I only wish I'd had it ready this morning."

"I don't think you'll have any cause to use it," Frank said reassuringly. "It was Jones they were after. They won't bother you again."

"They'd better not."

"I think the best thing we can do, Joe, is to go right back to Bayport and let dad know about this."

"Good idea. We can't do anything by staying here."

53

"You boys said yesterday that your name was Hardy, eh?" said the farmer. "Ain't any relation to Fenton Hardy, are you?"

"He's our father."

"The detective?"

The Hardy boys nodded assent.

"Good!" exclaimed Kane. "You go right back and tell him about this. If any one can get to the bottom of this affair it's him. I hate to see them rascals getting away scot-free."

Frank and Joe bade good-bye to the farmer and his wife and returned to their motorcycles. They promised to call again at the Kane farm as soon as they had any further information and Mr. Kane, in turn, gave his promise to notify them if there were any further trace of the kidnappers or of the mysterious Jones.

When they returned to Bayport the boys lost no time in reaching home. Fenton Hardy was enjoying one of his rare afternoons of leisure in reading, but he put his book aside when the boys rushed into the library.

"Did Mr. Jones talk?" he asked quickly, seeing by their expressions that something unusual had happened.

"We didn't have a chance to see him!" exclaimed Joe.

"What's the matter? Did he clear out?"

"He was kidnapped!"

"Kidnapped!"

"Four men broke into the farmhouse and took him away," said Frank hurriedly.

Then he proceeded to tell the story of the strange events of the morning at the Kane farm, prompted occasionally by Joe.

Mr. Hardy was deeply interested.

"There's only one theory I can think of," he said, at last. "This Jones, or whatever his name is, must have belonged to a gang and either squealed on them or threatened to do so. They tried to get rid of him and he escaped in the motorboat, but they thought they had finished him in the explosion. Then they found out that you had rescued him, so they went to the farmhouse and took him away before he had a chance to talk."

"Do you think they are smugglers?"

"Probably. While you were away this morning I called up one of the government authorities in the city, and he told me that they believe smugglers are operating in Barmet Bay on a big scale."

"Did you tell him about Snackley?"

Mr. Hardy smiled. "Not yet. That information, I thought I would keep to myself for the time being. But I wonder if Snackley can be here. It begins to look like it. He is the kind who wouldn't stop at anything from kidnapping to murder."

"Do the authorities suspect him of being around here?"

"I imagine so. The man I was talking to mentioned the fact that the smugglers they are after are in the drug line. And Snackley is king of the dope smugglers on the Atlantic coast."

"Gee! I wish we could land him."

"Of course," said Fenton Hardy, "no one has asked us to work on this case, and I don't believe in working for nothing—"

"You mean you won't help?" asked Joe, in disappointment.

Fenton Hardy's eyes twinkled as he went on.

"I don't believe in working for nothing," he repeated. "But if we ever caught this man Snackley it would be worth our while."

"Why?"

"The reward."

"Is there a reward offered for him?"

"There has been a standing reward of five thousand dollars offered for Snackley's capture for some time. And if he is operating in Barmet Bay, as I suspect, it's just possible that we might be able to collect that reward."

"Good!" exclaimed Frank. "Let's go after it!"

CHAPTER IX

THE STRANGE MESSAGE

The Hardy boys expected that the next day would find them busy on a more detailed investigation of the circumstances surrounding the mysterious kidnapping. But, to their surprise, when they came down to breakfast next morning they found that their father had gone away.

Mrs. Hardy could not enlighten them.

"He went out early this morning and didn't say when he would be back. But he didn't take any baggage with him, so I imagine he hasn't gone very far. He'll probably be back some time to-day."

Mrs. Hardy was accustomed to the comings and goings of her husband, and nothing surprised her. She realized that his profession demanded that he do many things that were mysterious enough on the surface but reasonable enough when the time came to explain them. But the boy were taken aback, for they had looked forward to seeing their father in the morning and had hoped that he would lay a plan of campaign before them. They went to school in

57

disappointment.

On the way they met Callie Shaw and Iola Morton, two girls who were particular friends of the boys. Callie Shaw, a brown-eyed, brown-haired girl was an object of special enthusiasm with Frank, who was apt to cast an appreciative eye upon the other sex, while Iola, a plump, dark girl, a sister of Chet Morton's, was "all right, as a girl," in Joe's reluctant opinion.

Chet had told his sister about the affair at the Polucca place on the previous Saturday, and she, in turn, had told Callie.

"Well, how are the ghost-hunters this morning?" asked Callie.

"Fine," replied Frank, with a smile.

"What a brave bunch of boys you all are!" exclaimed the girl. "Running away from an empty house!"

"That house wasn't empty!" put in Joe warmly. "I suppose you think our motorcycle tools walked away!"

"Somebody played a pretty good practical joke on you. Just wait till you get to school. Whoever played that trick will be sure to tell everybody."

"Oh, well, we can stand it. If Chet Morton hadn't been with us at the time I would have blamed him. It's like one of his pet ideas."

"He can prove an alibi this time," said Iola. "He was right with you, and by the way he talked when he got home I think he was as badly frightened as any one."

But when the boys reached school they found that although news of their experience at the house on the cliff had preceded them, no one was laying claim to having originated the joke. Chet and the other boys had told of the escapade but although they momentarily expected that some practical jester would come forward and take credit for the whole affair, nothing of the sort happened, and when noon came it was as much a mystery as ever.

"I'm beginning to think it wasn't a joke at all," admitted Joe, on the way home. "Believe me, if it had been a trick played on us the fellow who did it wouldn't have lost any time coming around to have the horselaugh."

"It was a little too well done to be a joke. I think some one started this ghost rumor just to keep people away from the Polucca place."

"If everybody gets the same reception we got, I don't blame 'em for staying away. What with weird yells and shrieks, with walls falling in and tool boxes being robbed, it's a mighty active ghost they have on the job."

"I wonder—could it have anything to do with the smugglers, Joe?"

The Hardy boys looked at one another.

"There's a thought!" exclaimed Joe. "We had two mighty strange things happen to us on the same day. Perhaps they *have* something to do with each other."

"It might be only a coincidence. But when you come to think of it, that house on the cliff would be a mighty handy hangout for smugglers if they could keep strangers away. And what better way than by starting a story that the place is haunted?"

"Gosh, I never thought of that! I wonder what dad thinks of it."

"Perhaps he's at home now. We'll mention it to him."

But when they returned home for lunch they found that Fenton Hardy had not come back. Neither was he at home when school closed for the day; and when the Hardy boys went to bed that night there had not been the slightest word from their father nor any indication of where he had gone. In spite of the fact that they were accustomed to these sudden absences, the lads felt vaguely uneasy.

"I don't know why," said Frank next morning, "but I have a sort of feeling that everything isn't all right."

"I've been feeling that way myself. Of course, dad has often gone away from home like this without telling where he was going, and he has always turned up all right. But this time—"

"Well, we'll just have to wait and see. He knows his own business best, and it's ten chances to one we're worrying over nothing, but I have a sort of a hunch that there's a nigger in the woodpile."

Mrs. Hardy, however, was not alarmed.

"Oh, he'll walk into the house when we're least expecting him," she laughed reassuringly. "You boys are just anxious to get to work on the Snackley case. Perhaps that's what he's working on now, he'll probably come back with a lot of information."

"We'd rather he'd let us in on that," returned Joe.

"And keep you out of school! Oh, no. He doesn't mind letting you do detective work as long as it's in your spare time."

So the Hardy boys had to make the best of it. They concealed their impatience during the remainder of the week doing their school work faithfully. The following week was the start of vacation, and the lads were deep in examination for several days so that they had not much time to think of detective activities.

But on Friday afternoon the mystery of their father's absence took a strange turn.

They came back from school to find their mother sitting in the living room, carefully examining a note that she had evidently just received.

"Come here, boys," she said, as they came into the room. "

want you to look at this and tell me what you think of it."

She handed the note over to Frank.

"What is it?" he asked, quickly. "Word from dad?"

"It's supposed to be."

The Hardy boys read the note. It was written in pencil on a torn sheet of paper and the handwriting seemed to be that of Fenton Hardy. The note read:

"I won't be home for several days. Don't
worry."

It was signed by the detective. That was all. There was nothing to indicate where he was, nothing to show when the note had been written.

"When did you get this?" asked Frank.

"It came in the afternoon mail. It was addressed to me, and the envelope had a Bayport postmark."

"What is there to worry about?" Joe asked. "It's better than not hearing from him at all."

"But I'm not sure that it's from him."

"Why?"

"Your father has an arrangement with me that he would always put a secret sign beneath his signature any time he had occasion to write to me like this. He was always afraid of people forging his name to letters and notes like this and perhaps getting papers or information that they shouldn't. So we arranged this sign that he would always put beneath his name."

Frank snatched up the note again.

"And there's no sign here. Just his signature."

"It *may* be his signature. If it isn't, it is a very good forgery. And it may have been that he forgot to put in the secret sign, although it isn't like him to do that."

Mrs. Hardy was plainly worried.

"If he didn't write it, then who did?" asked Joe.

"Your father has many enemies. There are relatives of criminals whom he has had arrested and there are criminals who have served their terms and have been released. If there has been foul play the note might be meant to keep us from being suspicious and delay any search."

"Foul play!" exclaimed Frank. "You don't think something has happened to dad?" he added, his face showing his alarm.

"The fact that he didn't put the secret sign underneath his name makes me anxious. What other object could any one have in sending us a note like that, if not to keep us from starting a search for him?"

"Well, whether he wrote that note or not, we *will* start a search for him," declared Frank firmly. "He merely said not to worry about him. He didn't order us not to look for him. If he really did write the note he can't say we were disobeying instructions. And then, the absence of the secret sign makes it all different."

"I'll say we'll look for him!" cried Joe. "Vacation starts next week, and we'll have plenty of time to hunt for him."

"Wait until then, at any rate," Mrs. Hardy advised. "Perhaps he will return in the meanwhile."

But as she glanced at the note again and once more regarded the signature, strangely lacking its secret sign, her forebodings that Fenton Hardy had met with foul play increased.

CHAPTER X

THE VAIN SEARCH

Fenton Hardy was still missing when the summer vacation began.

There had been no word from him. Never, in all his years of detective work, had he vanished from home so completely and for such a length of time. He was an intensely considerate man and his first thought was always for his wife and boys. Occasionally it was necessary for him to leave home suddenly on trips that would keep him away for some length of time, sometimes it seemed wiser to keep the knowledge of his whereabouts to himself. But he always managed to communicate with Mrs. Hardy to assure her of his safety.

But this time, with the exception of the dubious note, there had been no such assurance. From the moment he had left the house on the morning after the kidnapping at the Kane farmhouse he had vanished as utterly as though the earth had swallowed him up.

The Hardy boys questioned many people in and around

Bayport, but no one recollected having seen their father on the day in question. At the railway station they ascertained the fact that the detective had not bought a train ticket that day or any day since. The agent admitted it was barely possible that Fenton Hardy might have taken a train and paid his fare on board, but said it was not likely. Inquiries at the steamboat office brought a similar response. The detective had not been seen.

None of the local police officers remembered having seen Mr. Hardy that morning. The detective was a well-known figure in Bayport and it seemed strange that no one had seen him about the streets of the city, in spite of the fact that he had left home at an early hour. The boys questioned every one who was likely to have seen him, even to milkmen who might have been on their routes at that time, but the further they pursued their inquiries the deeper the mystery became.

One of the boys greatly interested in the disappearance of Mr. Hardy was Perry Robinson. Perry was the son of Henry Robinson, who had once gotten into difficulties over the disappearance of some valuables, as related in "The Tower Treasure." All of the Hardys had done much for the Robinson family, and the Robinsons were correspondingly grateful.

"I saw your dad on the street one day, boys," said Perry. "He waved his hand to me."

"When was that?" demanded Frank quickly.

"Oh, a day or two before you say he disappeared. Gee, fellows, I wish I could help you!" went on Perry.

"Well, keep your eyes open and if you learn anything let us know," said Joe, and to this Perry readily agreed.

Shortly after the boys had had their talk with Perry Robinson they ran into a number of their girl friends. One of these girls had likewise seen Mr. Hardy, but after considerable questioning the boys came to the conclusion that the meeting had taken place several days before their father's disappearance.

"Oh, I'm so sorry this happened," said one of the girls, and the others nodded in sympathy.

The Hardy boys extended the search beyond the city. It occurred to them that their father might have gone out to the Kane farm, and they made their way to that place. But the farmer and his wife said no one had called at the house since the eventful Sunday of the kidnapping.

"They've left us in peace, praise be!" declared Mrs. Kane. "No one's been near the house since those rascals went away."

The boys gave the kindly couple a description of their father, but Mr. Kane could not recollect having seen any one resembling Mr. Hardy near the farm at any time within the past week. He had been working in the fields, he said, and would probably have noticed any strangers on the road.

So the boys returned to Bayport, puzzled and downhearted over the failure of their search. They could not imagine where Fenton Hardy could have gone if he had not been near the Kane farm.

"Something has happened to him, I'm sure," said Frank. "It isn't like dad to stay away this long without sending some word."

"Perhaps he *did* write that note."

"He would have explained a little more. And he would have put in the secret sign."

The fact that the Hardy boys were searching for their father gradually became known throughout Bayport, and one evening a thick-set, broad-shouldered man presented himself at the front door of the Hardy home and asked for the boys. Mrs. Hardy bade him step inside and he waited in the hall, nervously twisting his cap in his hands.

When Frank and Joe came out the stranger introduced himself as Sam Bates.

"I'm a truck driver," he told them. "The reason I came around to see you was because I heard you were lookin' for your father."

"Have you seen him?" asked Frank eagerly.

Sam Bates shuffled his feet and looked dubiously at the floor.

"Well, I have and I haven't, you might say," he observed. "I *did* see your father quite a few days ago, but where he is now, I couldn't tell you, for I don't know." Sam was evidently not a man of gigantic intellect. He spoke slowly and painstakingly and his most obvious statements were delivered with the gravity suitable to pearls of wisdom.

"Where did you see him?"

"I'm a truck driver, see?"

"Yes, you told us that," said Frank impatiently. "But where did you see our father?"

Sam Bates was not to be hurried. He had a story to tell and he was bound to tell it.

"I'm a truck driver, see?" he repeated. "Mostly I drive just in and around Bayport, but sometimes they give me a run out to some of them villages. That's how I come to be out there that morning."

"Out where?"

"I'm comin' to that. I just forget what day it was, but I think it was about a week from last Monday. I know it was just after Sunday because when I went home to dinner that day the wife was washin' clothes and dinner was late and I had to eat it out on the back steps anyway for the kitchen was all in a mess. You know how it is on wash day."

Sam Bates regarded them wistfully, as though hoping for

some expression of sympathy and understanding. But the Hardy boys were eager for information, and impatient with the worthy truck driver's circuitous method of telling his story.

"But what has this got to do with our father?" demanded Joe.

"I'm comin' to that, see? Give me time. Give me time. As I was sayin', I'm pretty sure it was on a Monday, for it was wash day, and the wife never washes except on Monday. I mean she never washes clothes except on Monday. She herself, why, she washes *every* day, of course. Anyway, it was Monday."

"That was the day dad disappeared," prompted Frank.

"You don't say! Well, I saw him that day."

"Where?"

"I'm comin' to that. As I was sayin', it was Monday, and when I went down to the garage the boss, he says to me, says he, 'Sam, I want you to run a truckload of furniture down the shore road.' So I said, 'Well, boss, I guess that's what I'm here for,' so he told me that this here load of furniture had to go to one of them farmhouses away down near the Point. So we loaded the truck and I filled her up with gas and away I went. It must have been about nine o'clock by then I guess."

"And you went down the shore road?"

"Sure. And it was a nice mornin' for drivin' too. Anyway, I went out past the Tower Mansion—you know, Hurd Applegate's place, them people you and your father got back the Tower treasure for—and I was drivin' along without a care in the world and whistlin' away, quite happy-like, when I sees that I was comin' near that haunted house up on the cliff. You know the place—where old Polucca was murdered."

"The Polucca place!"

"Yeah! Well, anyway, I was comin' by there and I didn't drive slow either, for they say there's ghosts in that place and I ain't takin' no chance with nothin' like that, so the truck was going along at quite a clip, when what should I see but a man walkin' along the road."

"Dad!"

"Yeah, it was your father. Well, anyway, nobody ever said Sam Bates wouldn't give a guy a lift, so I slows down a bit and I says, 'Hey! D'you want a ride?' just like that, see? Then this guy turned around so I seen who it was. I didn't know until then, see? So when I seen who it was I said, 'Good day, Mr. Hardy, would you like a lift?' but he thanked me and said he was just takin' a little walk. So I drove on past him and the last I seen of him he was walkin' along beside the road."

"Did he go down the lane to the Polucca place?'

"I dunno whether he did or not. He hadn't quite reached the lane when I seen him last. But I didn't meet him on my way back, so I don't know where he went. Matter of fact, I didn't think nothin' more of it until this mornin' when a bunch of the boys were sittin' around the garage talkin' and one of them said that you two lads had been huntin' all over the city for your old man—I mean your father—and you couldn't find him. So I says to myself, 'Sam, mebbe you can tell 'em somethin' they don't know.' So I just thought I'd come up."

"And we're very grateful to you," Frank assured him. "You've given us some valuable information. We didn't know whether our father had gone out of the city or not. Now I think we'll know where to look for him."

"Ain't any chance of him nosin' around that Polucca place, is there?" asked Bates. "It's a mighty good place to stay away from if everythin' you hear is true. It's haunted, that place is."

"Oh, that wouldn't matter to him. But I'm glad you told us about seeing him. It gives us a better idea of where to look for him."

"Well, I'm glad if I've helped any. Guess I'll be goin' now," said Sam Bates, putting on his cap. "I hope your dad shows up all right."

The Hardy boys thanked him warmly and Bates shambled away, his hands in his pockets.

Mrs. Hardy came into the hallway.

"Any news?" she asked anxiously.

"We have a clue, anyway," Frank told her. "That fellow says he saw dad on the shore road the morning he left here."

"Where was he?"

"Near the old Polucca place."

"The house on the cliff?"

Frank nodded.

Mrs. Hardy looked grave. "Surely he couldn't have gone there and disappeared!" she said.

"I can't imagine why he would go to the house on the cliff, anyway," observed Joe.

"Oh, I know now!" Mrs. Hardy exclaimed. "I had forgotten all about it. I intended to tell you boys, but somehow it slipped my mind. Now that you mention the Polucca place, I remember."

"What was it?"

"Your father discovered something about Snackley, the smuggler. It seems that Snackley was related to Felix Polucca, the miser."

"Related to him!"

"He was a cousin or nephew, or something of the sort. One of the government men told him that. So your father had an idea that Polucca must have been visited by Snackley at some time or another and that Snackley must have got the idea of using Barmet Bay for his smuggling operations at that time."

"Whew!" exclaimed Joe. "Now we're getting on the right track. Dad must have gone up to the house on the cliff to investigate."

"Why didn't we think of searching there before! Dad put two and two together and figured that there might be some connection between the queer things that happened at the Polucca place the day we visited it and the case of that fellow Jones whom we rescued. Then, when he learned that Snackley was related to Polucca, he was sure of it. It's as clear as daylight. But what on earth could have happened to him?"

"Let's go up to the Polucca place and find out."

But Mrs. Hardy interposed. Her lips were firm.

"Promise me you won't go alone."

"Why not, mother? We can look after ourselves."

"If anything has happened to your father, I don't want you to run the same risk."

"But we *must* go up there and look the place over again."

"Get some of the boys to go with you."

"I guess it would be safer," agreed Joe. "We can round up a bunch of the fellows and go up there to-morrow morning. We'll search that place from top to bottom this time."

Mrs. Hardy gave her consent to this plan and the boys thereupon set out to find their chums and tell them of the proposed trip. Although two or three of the boys backed out when they learned that the destination was to be the haunted house, the majority were willing enough, and by nightfall all was in readiness for the journey on the morrow.

CHAPTER XI

THE CAP ON THE PEG

Next morning the searching party set out.

Jerry Gilroy had not got over the scare he had received on the remarkable Saturday of the boys' first visit to the house on the cliff and he did not show up. But Chet Morton and Biff Hooper appeared, with Phil Cohen and Tony Prito, two more of the Hardy boys' chums at the Bayport high school. Chet had his motorcycle and the party left the Hardy home shortly after breakfast, each machine carrying two.

Before they left, Frank explained the situation fully to the others.

"We know that dad was last seen near the Polucca place and we have every reason to believe that he left here with the intention of searching the house. He hasn't shown up since and no person has seen him, so there may have been foul play."

"If there is any trace of him around the Polucca place we'll find it," declared Chet. "It will take a mighty lively ghost to

71

scare us away this time."

The three motorcycles went out of Bayport past the Tower Mansion, sped along the shore road. There was little talk among the boys. Each realized that this was not a pleasure outing but a serious mission and each recognized the importance of it. The Hardy boys had every confidence in their companions. Chet and Biff, they knew, would not be as easily frightened on this occasion, and as for Phil and Tony, they were noted at school for their fearless, at times even reckless, dispositions.

They passed the Kane farmhouse, nestling among the trees, and at last came in sight of the gloomy cliff that rose from Barmet Bay and at the summit of which perched the rambling stone house where the miser, Felix Polucca, had met his death.

"Lonely looking place, isn't it?" remarked Phil, who was sharing Frank's motorcycle.

"It was an ideal place for a murder. When Felix Polucca lived there, I doubt if he had more than two or three visitors in a year."

"How did he get his food and supplies?"

"He used to drive into the city about once a week in a rattly old buggy, with a horse that must have come out of the Ark. The poor animal looked as if it hadn't had a square meal in a lifetime. Polucca must have been a little bit crazy. How he lived alone up there all the time, nobody could understand. He worked hard enough and he made the farm pay. No one could drive a better bargain when it came to selling his hay and grain."

Phil looked with interest at the old gray house that could be seen more clearly now that they were approaching it. When they were still some distance from the lane, however, Frank brought his motorcycle to a stop and signaled to the others to do likewise.

"What's the idea?" Chet asked.

"We'd better sneak up on the place quietly. If we go any farther they'll hear the motorcycles—that is, if there is any one at the place. We'll leave them here under the trees and go ahead on foot."

The motorcycles were accordingly hidden in a clump of bushes beside the road and the six boys went on toward the lane.

"We'll separate here," Frank decided. "Three of us will take one side of the lane and the rest will take the other side. Keep to the bushes as much as possible and when we get near the house lay low for a while and watch the place. When I whistle we can come out from under cover and go on up to the house."

"That's a good plan," approved Tony. "Joe and Biff and I, we'll go on the left side of the road."

"Good. Chet and Phil and I will take the other side. Remember to keep out of sight of the house as much as possible."

The boys entered the lane, then separated according to the agreement they had made. One group plunged into the weeds and undergrowth at the edge of the lane on one side while the others pushed into the bushes at the opposite side. In a few minutes each group was lost to view and only an occasional snapping and crackling of branches indicated their presence in the heavy undergrowth that flanked the lane.

Frank advanced cautiously. The brushwood was much deeper than he had anticipated and they made slow progress, for he was desirous of creeping up on the house with as little noise as possible. The undergrowth was thick and hampered their movements. They made their way forward, step by step, keeping well in from the lane, and after about ten minutes Frank raised his hand as a warning to the others.

73

Through the dense thickets he had caught a glimpse of the house.

They went on cautiously until they reached the edge of the bushes and there they crouched behind the screen of leaves, peeping out at the gloomy old stone building in the clearing.

But at the first glance, an expression of surprise crossed Frank's face.

The Polucca house was evidently occupied!

The weeds that had overgrown the yard on their last visit had been completely cleared away, the grass had been cut and the tumble-down fence had been repaired. The gate, which had been hanging by one hinge, had been fixed and the grass along the pathway had been trimmed.

A similar change had overtaken the house.

There was glass in all the windows and the boards had been removed. The front door had been repaired and the steps had been mended. Smoke was rising from the kitchen chimney.

"There must be some one living here," whispered Chet.

Frank was puzzled.

He had not heard that any one had taken the Polucca house. On account of the unenviable fame of the place it was hardly likely that a new tenant could move in without arousing considerable comment in Bayport. But this had evidently happened.

For a while the boys remained at the edge of the bushes watching the place. Then they saw a woman come out to the clothesline at the back of the house. She carried a basket of clothes, and these she began hanging up on the line. Shortly afterward a man came out, strode across the yard to the woodshed and began chopping wood.

The boys looked at one another in consternation.

They had expected to find the same sinister and deserted place they had visited previously. Instead, they had arrived on a scene of domestic peace and comfort. They could not understand it.

"Not much use staying in hiding," whispered Frank. "Let's get together and walk right up and question these people."

He gave a low whistle, then emerged from the bushes into the lane. His companions followed. In a short time they were joined by Joe and the other boys.

All were deeply puzzled by the remarkable change that had come over the Polucca place.

"This beats anything I ever heard of," declared Joe. "It looks as if some farmer has taken the place, but it's queer we hadn't heard of it. Everybody in Bayport would be talking about it if they knew some one had nerve enough to take over the Polucca farm."

"I'm not satisfied yet," Frank said. "We'll go up and question these people."

Accordingly, the six boys walked boldly out of the lane and across the yard. The man in the woodshed saw them first and put down his axe, staring at them with an expression of annoyance on his face. The woman at the clothesline heard their footsteps and turned, facing them, her hands upon her hips. She was hard-faced and tight-lipped, with gaunt features. She was not prepossessing and her untidy garb did not impress the boys favorably.

"What do you want?" demanded the man, emerging from the woodshed.

He was short and thin with close-cropped hair, and he was in need of a shave. His complexion was swarthy and he had narrow eyes under coarse, black brows. His manner was far from polite as he advanced upon the boys.

At the same time another man came out of the kitchen and

stood on the steps. He was stout and red-haired and had a thick mustache. As he stood there in his shirt-sleeves he glared pugnaciously at the sextette.

"Yeah, what's the big idea?" he asked.

"We didn't know any one was living here," explained Frank, edging over to the kitchen door. He wanted to get a look inside the house if possible.

"Well, there is," said the red-haired man. "We're livin' here now, and I can't see that it's any of your business. What are you snooping around here for?"

"We aren't snooping," said Frank quietly. "We are looking for a man who has disappeared from Bayport."

"Humph!" grunted the woman.

"What makes you think he might be around here?" asked the red-headed man.

"He was last seen in this neighborhood."

"What's his name?"

"Hardy."

"What does he look like?"

"Tall and dark. He was wearing a grey suit and a grey cap."

"Ain't been nobody around here since we moved in," said the red-headed man gruffly.

"No, we didn't see him," snapped the woman. "You boys had better go and look somewhere else."

There was nothing to be gained by arguing with the unsociable trio, so the boys started to leave. But Frank, who had edged close to the open door during the course of the conversation, had glanced into the kitchen and something had caught his eye.

It was a gray cap, hanging on a peg!

CHAPTER XII

POINTED QUESTIONS

Frank thought quickly. He must ascertain the truth!

The cap, he was almost sure, was the one his father had worn on the morning he had left home. But he wanted to look at it closely, because he knew he might be mistaken and that it would not do to make any accusations unless he were sure of his ground.

"I'm very thirsty," he said quickly. "Do you mind if I have a drink?"

Redhead and the woman looked at one another without enthusiasm. It was plain that they wished to get rid of their visitors as soon as possible. But they could not refuse such an innocent and reasonable request.

"Come into the kitchen," said Redhead grudgingly.

This was just what Frank wanted. He followed the man into the kitchen of the Polucca place. Redhead pointed to a water tap. A dipper was hanging from a nail near by.

"Go ahead," he grunted.

Frank went over to the tap and as he did so he passed the cap on the peg. He took a swift look at the cap.

He had made no mistake. It was his father's.

Then he received a shock that almost stunned him. For a second he almost stopped in his tracks, but then he recollected himself and moved mechanically on toward the tap.

He had seen bloodstains!

On the lower edge of the cap were three large stains, reddish in color. They could have been made by nothing but blood.

In a daze, Frank turned on the water, filled the dipper and drank. At last he turned away, conscious that Redhead had been eyeing him carefully all the time.

"Thanks," he said, and again cast a glance at the peg.

The cap was gone!

Redhead had undoubtedly snatched it away and hidden it. Frank gave no sign that he noticed anything amiss, and walked out of the kitchen into the yard, where he rejoined the others.

"I guess we may as well be going," he said.

"You might as well," snapped the woman. "There's been no strangers around here."

"We're sorry we troubled you," said Joe. "Good-bye."

Redhead grunted a curt farewell. The woman and the other man said nothing as the boys turned away and retraced their steps out to the lane. For a while they walked on in silence and then, when they were out of sight of the house, Frank turned to the others.

"Do you know why I went into the kitchen?" he asked.

"Why?" they demanded eagerly, and Joe put in:

"I thought there was something fishy about the way you asked for that drink. What did you see?"

"I saw dad's cap hanging on a peg!"

This caused an immediate sensation. Phil Cohen whistled in amazement.

"Then he *has* been here! They were lying!"

"Are you sure it was dad's cap?" asked Joe.

"Positive. I'd recognize it anywhere. And more than that, there were bloodstains on it."

"Bloodstains!"

Frank nodded.

The boys looked at one another in silence.

"This is serious," declared Joe finally. "We can't let them get away with this."

"I'll say we can't," agreed Chet. "Let's go back."

"I was going to argue it out right there and then, but I thought I'd better tell the rest of you first so that you'd know what it was all about," Frank explained.

"He may have been—" Joe left the sentence unfinished.

"He may have been murdered," said Frank firmly. "And we're going to find out about it."

"What do you think we'd better do?"

"I think we'd better go back and tell them we saw that cap and ask how it got there. That'll force a showdown. They don't like us any too well as it is, so we won't have to be over polite to them."

The boys held a council, and it was unanimously agreed that the matter should not be dropped. Each was of the opinion that the trio now occupying the house on the cliff were far from savory and that the fact of Fenton Hardy's cap being seen in the kitchen was a clue of first-rate importance.

"He snatched the cap away when my back was turned," went on Frank.

"That shows there is something wrong," Chet affirmed. "We'll go back and tackle him right away."

"No time like the present. Let's go."

The boys accordingly started back down the lane toward the house. When they emerged into the yard again they found the two men and the woman standing together by the shed, talking earnestly. The boys were almost up to them before the woman caught sight of them and spoke warningly to the red-headed man.

"What do you want now?" demanded Redhead, in a surly manner, as he advanced.

"We want to know about that cap in the kitchen," said Frank firmly.

"What cap? There's no cap in there."

"There isn't now—but there was. It's a grey cap and it was hanging in there when I went in for a drink."

"I don't know anythin' about no cap," persisted Redhead.

"Perhaps you want us to ask the police up to help us find out," put in Tony Prito cheerfully.

Redhead glanced meaningly at the woman. The other man stepped forward.

"I know the cap he means," he said. "It's mine. What about it?"

"It isn't yours, and you know it," declared Frank. "That cap belongs to the man we're looking for."

"I tell you it *is* my cap," snapped the swarthy man, showing his yellow teeth in a snarl. "Don't tell me I'm lying."

Redhead stepped forward diplomatically.

"You're mistaken, Klein," he said. "I know the cap they mean. That's the one I found on the road a few days ago."

"You found it?" asked Frank incredulously.

"Sure, I found it. A grey cap—with bloodstains on it."

"That's the one. But why did you hide it when I went into the kitchen?"

"Well, to tell the truth, them bloodstains made me nervous. I didn't know but what there might be some trouble come of it, so I thought I'd better keep that cap out of sight."

"Where did you find it?" Joe demanded.

"About a mile from here."

"On the shore road?"

"Yes. It was lying right in the middle of the road."

"When was this?"

"A couple of days ago—just after we moved in here."

"Let's see the cap," suggested Chet Morton. "We want to make sure of this."

Redhead moved reluctantly toward the kitchen. The woman sniffed.

"I don't see why you're makin' all this fuss about an old cap," she said. "Comin' around at this hour of the day disturbin' honest folk."

"We're sorry to disturb you, ma'am," said Joe. "But this is a serious matter."

Redhead emerged from the house holding the cap in one hand. He tossed it over to the boys. They examined it eagerly.

Frank turned back the inside flap and there he found what he was looking for—the initials F.H. imprinted in indelible ink on the leather band.

"It's dad's cap, all right."

"I don't like the look of those bloodstains," said Joe, in a low voice. "He must have been badly hurt."

To tell the truth, the inside of the cap gave evidence that the wearer had been severely injured, for the bloodstains were of large extent. The boys examined them gravely.

"Are you sure you found this on the road?" Frank asked doubtfully.

"You don't think I'd lie about it, do you?"

"We can't very well contradict you. I don't mind telling you that we're going to turn this over to the police. This man has disappeared, and by the appearance of this cap he has met with foul play. If you know anything about it you'd better speak up now."

"He doesn't know anything about it," shrilled the woman angrily. "Go away and don't bother us. Didn't he tell you he found the cap on the road? Why should he know anythin' more about it than that?"

"We're going to take the cap with us."

"Take it," snapped Redhead. "I don't want it."

The boys turned away. Nothing further was to be gained by questioning the trio in the yard, and at any rate the lads had gained possession of the cap.

"We'd better go," said Frank in a low voice.

They went back toward the lane. As they entered it they cast a last glance back at the yard.

The woman and the two men were standing just where they had left them. The woman was motionless, her hands on her hips. Redhead was standing with his arms folded and the swarthy man was leaning on the axe.

All three were gazing intently and silently after the departing boys.

CHAPTER XIII

A PLAN OF ATTACK

Back in Bayport the boys discussed their visit to the house on the cliff from all angles.

None was satisfied with the explanation the red-headed man had given about the presence of the bloodstained cap in the house.

"I'm sure he knows more about it than he cares to tell," declared Frank.

"The other chap started to claim it at first, and then he stepped in with his story," Chet pointed out.

"That's the most suspicious part of it. And then, when I went into the kitchen in the first place, why should he have hidden the cap?"

"It's a mighty mysterious thing," Joe said. "The fact that dad has disappeared and the fact that there are bloodstains on that cap—"

"We ought to turn it over to Chief Collig," suggested Phil.

The boys looked at one another doubtfully. Chief of Police Collig was a fat, pompous official who had never been blessed by a super-abundance of brains. His chief satellite and aide-de-camp was Oscar Smuff, a detective of the Bayport police force. As Chet was fond of remarking, "If you put both their brains together you'd have enough for a half-wit."

"I don't think it would do much good," said Frank. "But it wouldn't do any harm either. Collig might be able to throw a scare into them, anyway, if he went up to that house and began asking questions."

The boys, therefore, trooped down to the police station and, after stating their business to the desk sergeant, were admitted to the chief's private office. They found Chief Collig and Detective Smuff deep in a game of checkers.

"It's your move, Smuff," said the chief. "What is it, boys?" he demanded, looking up.

Frank, producing the bloodstained cap, explained how and where it had been found. Smuff, in the meantime, scratched his head diligently for a while, then captured one of his opponent's kings.

Chief Collig grunted, whether in disappointment at the loss of the king or in acknowledgment of the information about the cap, the boys could not say.

"So it's Fenton Hardy's cap, eh?" asked the chief.

"It's his, all right."

"And what do you think has happened to him?"

"We don't know. That's what we want you to help find out. But, by the look of this cap, we're afraid there's been foul play."

"Just a minute, Smuff—just a minute." The chief contemplated the checkerboard for a few minutes, then made a move. He settled back in his chair. "Now try and beat *that*!" he said, and looked up at the boys again. "What do you want me to do?" he inquired.

"Help us find him."

The chief regarded them benevolently.

"Mebbe he'll show up in a day or so."

"He's been missing long enough already," protested Joe. "We want you to go up to the Polucca place and question those people. They know more about the affair than they care to tell."

"The Polucca place!" exclaimed the chief, pursing his lips. "We-ll, you see, it ain't in the city limits."

"But Fenton Hardy is a Bayport citizen."

"What d'you think about it, Smuff?"

"Just a minute—it's my move." Smuff meditated over the checkerboard for a while, made his move, then looked up judicially. "To tell you the truth, chief," he said, "I think we'd be just as well stayin' away from that Polucca place. There's been queer stories about it."

"That's what I think," agreed the chief.

"Do you mean to say you won't help us look for him?" exclaimed Frank.

"Oh, we'll keep our eyes open," the chief promised. "But he'll show up all right. He'll show up. Don't worry."

"He'll never show up if we wait for the Bayport Police Department to get into action," declared Chet warmly.

"Is *that* so?" said Chief Collig, nettled.

"Of course, chief," said Frank smoothly, "if you're afraid to go up to the Polucca place just because it's supposed to be haunted, don't bother. We can tell the newspapers that we believe our father has met with foul play and that you won't bother to look into the matter, but don't let us disturb you at all—"

"What's that about the newspapers?" demanded the chief, getting up from his chair so suddenly that he upset the checkerboard over Smuff's lap. "Don't let this get into the papers." The chief was constantly afraid of publicity unless it was of the most favorable nature.

"The taxpayers mightn't like it," suggested Joe. "They pay you to enforce the law and if they know you're afraid to go up to the Polucca place—"

"Now, now," said the chief nervously. "Who said anythin' about being afraid of the Polucca place? Can't you take a joke? Of course I'll go up and investigate this—at least I'll send Smuff up—"

"Who, me?" demanded Smuff, in alarm.

"Smuff and me, we'll go up together."

"I'm doggone sure I won't go up alone," declared Smuff.

"Well, as long as we're sure you'll investigate, we won't say anything to the newspapers," said Frank, and Chief Collig breathed a sigh of relief.

"That's fine. That's fine," he said. "Smuff and me, we'll go up there first thing to-morrow morning and if we find out anything we'll let you know."

But although Chief Collig and Detective Smuff duly departed from Bayport the next morning in an exceptionally noisy and decrepit flivver, with Smuff perched nervously at the wheel, they returned before noon with the news that they had been able to discover nothing further regarding Fenton Hardy. They had, they said, called at the house, but the people there had given a reasonable explanation as to the finding of the cap.

"Real nice people, they were too," added Chief Collig. "The man said he found the cap on the road, and why should he tell a lie about it? So Smuff and me, we came away."

"Yes," agreed Smuff profoundly, "we came away."

"In a hurry," suggested Joe sarcastically.

Collig and Smuff looked uncomfortable. To tell the truth they had been so impressed by the fearful stories they had heard of the house on the cliff that they had stayed no longer than was necessary. They had merely asked a few perfunctory questions of Redhead, had received his explanation of the finding of the cap, and had then hastened from the farm as quickly as was consistent with dignity.

"We've done our duty," declared Chief Collig. "No man can do more."

And with that the boys had to be content.

But they were not satisfied.

"There's some connection between this smuggling outfit and the house on the cliff," declared Frank. "This man Snackley is mixed up in all this, I'm sure."

"Didn't mother say he was related to Felix Polucca?"

"Yes—and isn't it likely that he inherited the Polucca farm after the old miser died? Perhaps that's what encouraged him to move his smuggling operations here."

"Perhaps Snackley was one of the two men we saw at the farm."

"I wouldn't be surprised," said Frank. "But what I'm thinking of is this—where did these two motorboats come from that day Jones was shot? We didn't see them out in the bay. They seemed to come right out from under the cliff."

"Do you mean you think there is a secret harbor in there?"

"There might be. Look at it this way. Snackley was the man

who "got" Jones that day, as he said. Snackley was related to Polucca, and may now own the farm. Snackley has been smuggling in Barmet Bay from some base that the government men have been unable to find. Perhaps that base is the Polucca farm."

"But it's on top of the cliff!"

"There may be a secret passage from the house to some hidden harbor at the foot of the cliff."

"Gosh, Frank, it sounds reasonable!"

"And perhaps that explains why the kidnappers got away with Jones so quickly that day. If they left the Kane farmhouse just a little while before we did, we should have been able to get within sight of them, anyway. But we didn't."

"You mean they turned in at the Polucca place?"

"Why not? Probably Jones is hidden there right now. That is—if they haven't killed him," he added hesitatingly.

"But what could have happened to dad?"

"That's what we're going to find out. What do you say to asking Tony if his father will lend us his motorboat and let us investigate the foot of that cliff?"

"What do you expect to find?"

"We'll find out if there's any place where motorboats could be hidden. And if we get any information we can turn it over to the government officials and have the Polucca place raided. Then we'll get some satisfaction out of it, anyway, and perhaps find out what happened to dad."

CHAPTER XIV

PRIVATE PROPERTY

The Hardy boys explained their plan to Tony Prito, who promised to ask his father about the motorboat provided they allowed him to go with them.

"I wouldn't miss it for anything," he said. "You let me come along on this trip with you and I'll see that we get the boat."

"We wouldn't go without you, Tony," promised Frank.

"I'll have the boat to-morrow afternoon. Be at the boathouse."

Tony was as good as his word. When Frank and Joe appeared at the little boathouse, one of a long row of ramshackle buildings along the shore, next afternoon, they found Tony clad in a greasy suit of overalls, tinkering with the engine. He was of a mechanical turn of mind and could never see an engine of any kind without investigating its most intricate machinery.

"She'll run as smoothly as a sewing machine," he declared looking up. "We can start any time."

"Your father let you have the boat, all right."

"You bet. I told him it was to help find your father, and he was almost going to quit work and come along with us."

The boys got into the motorboat, which was a rangy, powerful craft with graceful lines, and the engine was soon roaring. The boat, which was called the *Napoli* in honor of Mr. Prito's birthplace in Italy, moved slowly out into the waters of the bay and then gathered speed as it headed toward the gloomy cliffs at the northern extremity of Barmet Bay.

It was already late in the afternoon. The sky was overcast and the bay was rough. The salt spray dashed over the bows of the *Napoli* as it plunged on through the breakers. Bayport soon became a smoky haze on the hillside. The boys could see the white line of the shore road rising and falling on the coast to the north and at last they came within sight of the Kane farm, nestled among the trees.

The cliff upon which the Polucca place stood was stark and sheer against the background of ocean and sky, and at the top they could see the grove of trees and the roof and chimneys of the haunted house.

"Lonely looking place," remarked Joe.

"Pretty steep cliff," Tony observed. "I can't see how any one could make his way up and down that slope to get to the house."

"That's just why nobody has thought of the possibility of the place as a smuggling base," said Frank, "It doesn't look possible. But perhaps when we look around we'll find that things are different."

Tony steered the boat closer in toward the shore so that it would not be visible from the Polucca place. Then he slackened speed so that the roar of the engine would not be so noticeable, and the craft made its way along toward the bottom of the cliff.

There were currents here that demanded skilful navigation, but Tony brought the *Napoli* through them easily and at last the boat was surging along close to the face of the cliff. The boys scanned the formidable wall of rock eagerly.

It was scarred and seamed and at the base had been eaten away by the battering of the waves. Time passed, and there was no indication of a path and the lads were disappointed.

The cliff jutted up out of very deep water and rose to a great height. From the boat they were unable to see the Polucca place, for it was set in a short distance from the edge of the cliff. The face of the steep rock was uncompromising. There seemed to be no foothold for man or beast. It was just an unscalable, craggy wall.

Suddenly Tony bore down on the wheel. The *Napoli* swerved swiftly to one side and at the same time the engine roared as the craft leaped ahead.

Frank and Joe looked quickly around.

"What's the matter?" they asked, in alarm.

But Tony was gazing fixedly ahead. He was tense and alert. Another shift of the wheel and the *Napoli* swerved again.

Then the Hardy boys saw the danger.

There were rocks at the base of the cliff. One of them, black and sharp, like an ugly tooth, jutted out of the water almost immediately at the side of the boat. Only Tony's quick eye had saved them from striking against it. They had blundered into a veritable maze of reefs which extended for several yards ahead.

They held their breath.

It seemed impossible that they could run the gauntlet of those rocks without tearing the bottom out of the craft. But Tony's steermanship was marvelous. The motorboat threaded its way accurately among the jutting rocks. There was always the chance that a submerged reef might rip through the hull of the craft, but they had to take chances on that.

But luck was with them. The *Napoli* dodged the last ugly rock, and shot forward into open water.

Tony sank back with a sigh of relief.

"Whew, that was close!" he exclaimed. "I didn't see those rocks until we were right on top of them. If we'd ever struck one of them we would have been goners."

The Hardy boys believed him. Angry waves dashed against the base of the cliff. They would not have lived more than a few minutes if they had been wrecked in this place. They would have been battered to pieces against the rocks.

Suddenly, before them, they saw an opening in the side of the cliff. It was a long, narrow cove.

The entrance was like the neck of a bottle, widening as it led into the cliff, and it was over-shadowed by jutting rocks. It had been quite invisible up to this time, and the boat had gone only a few yards further before it became invisible again, so well was the opening hidden by the rocks.

"Here's a find!" exclaimed Frank, in excitement. "Let's turn back and see where this goes to."

Tony swung the boat around and the craft slowly made its way back toward the hidden cove. Soon the opening in the cliff came into view again.

"It's just large enough for the boat to go through," said Tony. "Want me to try it?"

Frank nodded.

"Go ahead."

The nose of the boat turned toward this strange bay and then the *Napoli* began to enter the cove.

"Maybe I won't be able to get out again," said Tony suddenly. He looked ahead. But the passage widened into a bay of considerable extent, quite sufficient in size to enable him to turn the craft around once he had entered. So he continued.

But the cove proved uninteresting. The sides were steep, although dense bushes grew about the base of the slopes, but there was no path, no trail, no indication that any human being had ever been in the place. Being protected from the wind, the water was calm. The echoes of the motorboat's engine were flung back from every side in a roaring volume.

Suddenly Frank gave a gasp of surprise!

Standing among the thickets at the base of the steepest slope, was a man.

He was very tall and he wore a black felt hat, the wide brim of which obscured the upper part of his face. His countenance was tanned and weatherbeaten, his lips were thin and cruel. He wore a short black jacket, and he stood with his hands plunged into the side-pockets and his feet spread wide apart, in the manner of a seaman.

He was standing there quietly, gazing at them without a shadow of expression on his sinister face, as motionless as a statue.

When he saw that he was observed he called out:

"Leave this place!"

Tony throttled down the engine. The three boys stared at the man in the black hat as though he were an apparition.

"Leave this place!" he repeated, in a curiously metallic voice.

"We aren't doing any harm," replied Frank.

"Not now," said the stranger. "But don't land here."

"Why?"

"You don't have to ask why. This is private property. You can't land here. You'd better leave at once."

The boys hesitated. As though to emphasize his commands, the man in the black hat reached suddenly into his pocket and whipped out a wicked-looking revolver. Then he folded his arms, tapping the barrel of the revolver against one shoulder very deliberately.

"Turn that boat around and get out of here!" he snapped. "Don't come back. Don't ever come back. Don't ever try to land here. This is private property. If you ever *do* land here you'll be shot."

The boys were unarmed. They realized that nothing would be gained by argument. Tony slowly brought the boat around.

"Good-bye," shouted Joe cheerfully.

The stranger did not reply. He stood there, gazing fixedly after them, his arms still folded, still tapping the revolver against his shoulder as the motorboat made its way out of the strange bay, out into open water.

"Looks as if he didn't want us around," remarked Tony, as soon as the *Napoli* was out of the cove.

"I'll say he didn't!" exclaimed Frank. "What a wicked-looking customer he was! I expected to see him start popping at us with that gun of his before we got out."

"I don't want to run into *him* again," Joe declared. "He sure gave us our orders. And he meant 'em, too."

"I wonder who he is," said Tony.

"Do you think—Fellows! do you think it could have been Snackley?" shouted Frank.

CHAPTER XV

SMUGGLERS

The thought struck Frank Hardy like a thunderbolt!

The appearance of the stranger had been so sinister, he was so evidently a lawless and desperate man who was accustomed to being obeyed, and his presence in this place indicated too clearly that he had some connection with the house on the cliff, that Frank's deduction seemed quite logical.

"Snackley!" exclaimed Joe. "It *must* be him."

"The head of the smugglers!"

"I've never seen a picture of Snackley and I've never heard him described," said Joe. "But that fellow looks just as I had pictured Snackley would look."

"He's a leader of some kind—you can tell that by his manner," put in Tony Prito.

"He's the fellow who chased Jones that day in the motorboat."

"And he'll chase us, too," declared Tony, "if we don't get away from here pretty quick."

"Why should we go now?" demanded Frank. "We've stumbled on something important. That may be the smugglers' cove."

"But how do they get to the house if you think they have anything to do with the Polucca place?" asked Tony. "Those cliffs in there are mighty steep."

"There must be some way that we don't know of. What do you say we hang around here for a while and see what we can do?"

Tony became infected with the enthusiasm of the Hardy boys and he readily agreed to keep the motorboat in the vicinity of the cliff, although it was decided that they should not remain too near, but cruise up and down the shore in case the sharp-eyed man should be watching them.

"It was a good thing we didn't put up an argument with that fellow," said Frank, at last.

"I'll say it was!" Tony agreed emphatically. "We didn't have much chance to argue with that revolver he had."

"I don't mean that. He may think we were just out for a cruise and accidentally wandered into that cove. If he knew we were hunting for dad he might have acted very differently."

"That's true, too," said Joe. "Well, we won't go home just yet."

It was late in the afternoon. The sky was overcast and twilight was falling. A cold wind blew in from the sea.

The motorboat went some distance down the shore and then they turned and, keeping well out in the bay, went on up past the cliff once again. They kept a sharp eye on the location of the cove, and in spite of the fact that they knew just where it was they were scarcely able to distinguish the narrow opening in the rocks.

"No wonder the place hasn't been heard of more often!" Frank said. "It looks like an unbroken wall of rock from this far out."

"You've got to be careful around here, Tony," cried Joe. "First thing you know we'll hit the rocks and be smashed."

"That's right," added Frank. "It's pretty dangerous so close to the cliff."

"You leave it to me," came from their schoolmate. "I know how to handle this boat."

It was true, Tony did know how to handle the motorboat; yet several times they came perilously close to the rocks over which the waves were dashing. In fact, once there came a slight bump followed by a grating sound which made the hearts of all the boys leap into their mouths.

"Narrow squeak, that," admitted Tony. "I guess I'd better keep out a little farther, after all."

"I certainly should," answered Frank.

Although they cruised around for more than an hour, they saw not the slightest sign of life either about the base of the cliff or on the Polucca place, which, keeping well out from shore as they did, they could plainly distinguish. As the gloom deepened they felt that it was almost useless to continue, but Frank decided that they should wait a while longer.

"These fellows aren't likely to move around much in daylight. Night is the time for their operations," he pointed out. "We'll hang around for a while longer."

Twilight deepened into darkness and the lights of Bayport could be seen as a yellow haze through the mist at the distant extremity of the bay. The cliff was but a dark smudge in the night and the waves broke against the rocks with a lonely sound.

Suddenly, through the darkness, they heard a muffled sound. Their own boat was running along quietly and they listened.

"Another boat," remarked Tony, in a whisper.

It was, indeed, another motorboat, and it was near the base of the cliff. At last they could distinguish a faint light, and toward this light they began to move slowly.

They were tense with excitement. Everything might depend on the events of the next few minutes.

When they had gone in toward the cliff as far as they dared, creeping up from the west, they could make out the gloomy outline of the other motorboat, which was making its way slowly out of the very face of the cliff itself.

At first they could not imagine how the craft had got in so close nor where it was coming from. They crept up closer, at imminent danger of discovery, and at imminent danger of being washed ashore on the rocks. Then, finally, they heard the other boat slow down, heard the faint clatter of oars, then voices.

After that, with an abrupt roar that startled them, the other motorboat suddenly plunged on out into the bay. They could hear it threshing on its way out toward sea at an ever-increasing rate of speed.

"Where is it going?" said Tony, in amazement.

Frank cautioned for silence.

"There's a rowboat around here," he whispered. "Lay low."

They waited in silence and at last they heard the rattle of oars again.

This time the sound was closer.

The rowboat was drawing near.

Fortunately the wind was from the sea and it blew the sounds toward them, at the same time keeping the men in the boat from hearing the muffled murmur of their own craft.

The rattle of oars continued and at last the boys could see the dim shape of the boat through the gloom. Finally they could distinguish the words of the dark figures in the craft. At a sign from Frank Tony cut off the engine for the time being.

But they could not make out complete sentences. The wind would whisk toward them a fragment of speech and then the rest of the words would be drowned.

"—three hundred pounds—" they heard a harsh voice saying, and then the rest of the sentence was lost.

A dull murmur of voices. Finally—

"I don't know. It's risky—"

The wind died for a moment and then through the gloom the boys saw that the rowboat was heading directly in toward the face of the cliff. It was not many yards away and as it passed by they heard the harsh voice again.

"Li Chang's share—" he was saying.

"No, we mustn't forget that," they heard a gruff voice reply.

"I hope they get away all right."

"What are you worrying about? Of course they'll get away."

"We've been watched, you know."

"It's all your imagination. Nobody suspects."

"Those boys at the house—"

"Just kids. If they come nosing around again we'll knock one of 'em on the head."

"I don't like this rough stuff. It's dangerous."

"We've got to do it or we'll end up in the pen. You can't be white-livered in this game. What's the matter with you to-night? You're nervous."

"I'm worried. I've got a hunch that we'd better clear out of here."

"Clear out!" replied the other contemptuously. "Are you crazy? Why, this place is as safe as a church. We can make a big clean-up before they know we're in this part of the country at all."

"Well, maybe you're right," said the first man doubtfully. "But still—"

His voice died away as the boat went on into the cove.

The boys could hear the rattle of oars and then a dull swishing of bushes, a muttered voice, and then silence fell.

The boys looked at one another through the gloom.

"Smugglers!" exclaimed Frank.

"Sounds mighty like it," replied Tony. "What do you think we should do?"

"Follow them."

"Sure," Joe agreed. "Follow them right into the cove."

But Tony demurred, though as he spoke he started up the engine again.

"Count me out," he said. "I don't like that talk about being knocked on the head. I may be foolish, but I'm not *that* foolish."

"There are three of us."

"And we don't know how many more of them. And they're grown men. I don't want to be trapped in that cove. Besides, the motorboat makes too much noise. They'd hear us coming and then we'd be done for."

This phase of the matter had not occurred to the Hardy boys, but they saw that it was reasonable. In the darkness it would be risky entering the narrow passage to the cove and then, as Tony said, it was probable that their approach would be heard.

"I hate to let them get away when we've got such a clue as this," said Frank. "There's no doubt they are smugglers. The men in that motorboat probably are going out to a ship for a cargo of smuggled goods, or else they have delivered a cargo and are on their way back."

"But where on earth did the motorboat come from!" exclaimed Joe. "There wasn't any boat in the cove when we were in there."

"Probably well hidden," said Frank. "There were a lot of bushes growing close down to the water's edge, I noticed. They'd have some sort of a hiding place fixed up."

"But where did all those men come from?"

"That's what we're going to find out. There must be some connection between this cove and the house on the cliff. I'm going ashore."

"Somebody's got to stay with the motorboat," said Tony. "I'm not afraid to go in there, and if it comes to a dare, I will go, although I don't want to be killed. But we can't leave the boat here, that's certain."

"I'll tell you what to do," said Frank. "Let Joe and me go ashore. Then we'll try to follow those men in the boat and see where they go. If we let them slip out of our hands now we may lose them altogether."

"And shall I wait?"

"No. You go back to Bayport and get help—lots of it."

"The police?"

"The federal men. Tell them we're on the track of the

smugglers. If Joe and I discover anything we'll wait here at the entrance to the cove and put the police on the right track when they get here."

"Good!" said Tony. "I'll put you ashore right away."

"Don't go too close or you'll wreck the boat. Joe, I guess you and I will have to swim ashore. Then we'll go around into the cove and find out all we can."

Tony edged the boat in as close to the gloomy shore as he could, and then, with a whispered farewell, the Hardy boys slipped over the side into the water. They were only a few yards from the rocks and after a short swim they emerged, dripping, on the mainland. They looked back. They could see the dim shape of the motorboat as it turned away and then they could hear its dull chugging as Tony Prito turned the craft back in the direction of Bayport.

"Now!" whispered Frank. "Now for the smugglers!"

CHAPTER XVI

THE SECRET PASSAGE

It was very dark.

"I wish we had a light," whispered Joe.

"I have a flashlight in my pocket. But we can't use it now. Those men may be still around."

"Wouldn't the water spoil it?"

"No; I have it in a waterproof case. We can feel our way around these rocks until we get into the cove."

Cautiously, the boys made their way along the treacherous rocks. Once Joe lost his footing and slipped into the water with a splash. Instantly both boys remained motionless, fearing the sound had attracted the attention of the men in the cove. But there was not a sound.

Joe was ankle-deep in water, but he clambered up on the rocks again and they continued their journey.

They had landed at a point some twenty-five yards away from the entrance to the cove, but the rocks were so treacherous and the journey was so difficult that the distance seemed much longer.

"It must be Snackley and his gang, all right," whispered Frank, as they went on through the night. "Didn't you hear one of those men use a Chinese name?"

"He said something about Li Chang's share."

"Li Chang is probably the fellow who brings the dope to the coast. They bring the stuff into this cove by motorboat and rowboat and it is distributed from here. Dad said Snackley was smuggling dope."

"It must have been Snackley who ordered us away from here. He seemed like a leader of some kind."

"Five thousand dollars reward if we lay our hands on him!"

They had now reached the place where the seemingly solid coast line was broken by the indentation of the cove. They had feared that the cliff might be too steep at this point, but they found that it sloped gradually to the water and that there was a narrow ledge on which they could walk, one behind the other.

Here, they realized, the dangerous part of the adventure began.

It was very lonely in the shadow of the steep cliffs, and the loneliness was intensified by the distant moaning of the surf and the beat and wash of the waves against the reefs. Far in the distance they could see the reflection of the lights of Bayport through the mist and once or twice they could hear the murmur of Tony's motorboat as it sped away down the bay.

"I hope they bring back lights and guns with them," muttered Frank.

"Who?"

"The police."

"Don't worry. If they get word that Snackley is cornered they'll send out a squad of militia."

The boys rounded the point and began to make their way directly along the shore of the cove. Dense thickets and bushes grew right to the water's edge and the boys were afraid of making too much noise, as they realized that the two men they had heard talking in the boat might be close by—perhaps even waiting to pounce upon them in the darkness.

Their hearts beat quickly with the knowledge of the risk they were running, but neither lad thought of turning back. They were not thinking of the smugglers alone—they were thinking of their father.

When they reached the first of the thickets they paused. They knew that the crackling of the branches would betray their whereabouts if there was any one within hearing distance. For a while they did not know just what to do. Then Frank began to lower himself from the rock on which he was standing into the water.

"If it isn't too deep we can wade around," he whispered.

The water, fortunately, was shallow, and did not come up to his knees. He signaled to Joe to follow, and Joe accordingly slipped quietly down into the water beside him.

Then, without a word and moving as slowly as possible, Frank went on, wading through the water, close to the outstretched branches that overhung the shore.

It seemed as though they were wading at the bottom of a deep pit, for the high walls of rock ranged all about them and after they had penetrated into the cove some little distance the entrance was lost to view, being hidden by an angle of the cliffs. When they looked up they could see the gloomy greyness of the night sky above.

The cove was still in deep silence, so finally Frank concluded that the men who had entered the place in the boat had retired to some secret hiding place. Inasmuch as they could not hope to discover anything without a light, he withdrew the flashlight from its case, and then switched it on.

The yellow beam of light revealed the pallid leaves of the bushes by the shore and the naked walls of rock above. But although Frank turned the flashlight in every direction about the cove there was no sign of the rowboat in which the two men had arrived.

It had vanished utterly.

Although the lads were prepared for the disappearance of the smugglers, they were not prepared for the disappearance of the rowboat. But they searched for it in vain. The light revealed nothing of the craft.

"I wonder where they hid it!" whispered Frank.

They began a systematic search of the bushes around the cove, remaining as quiet as possible, but although they made almost a tour of the place it was soon evident that the boat had not been beached under cover of any of the thickets.

"It must be hidden in a cave of some kind," Frank decided at last. "And that's where the smugglers are."

Once again they began a search of the bushes.

They were still wading in the water and their feet were now very cold, but they searched patiently and carefully, brushing aside the branches, peering into the bushes, but it seemed they were to find nothing but the uncompromising rocks and moss beyond.

At last, however, as they were approaching a part of the cove which they had not visited before, Frank, who was in the lead, stumbled suddenly forward. His groping feet had failed to encounter bottom and he had lost his balance.

With great presence of mind, he kept the flashlight high in

the air. He had stepped into a deep hole, and although he was up to his neck in water he kept his arm raised, keeping the flashlight free of the wetness.

"Here! Take the light," he gasped, in a hoarse whisper.

Joe leaned over and grasped the flashlight.

"Deep water here," muttered Frank, as he tried to scramble back into the shallows.

But the hole into which he had fallen was a sudden drop and it was necessary for Joe to grasp his brother's outstretched hand before he could regain the shallow water. At length, soaked to the skin, Frank again stood beside his brother.

"Good thing it wasn't any deeper," he remarked.

"The bottom is pretty level around here. It's funny there should be a deep hole like that."

Frank gave a sudden exclamation.

"I know how that came to be there," he whispered. "That's a channel! See how close it is to the shore. The water shouldn't be so deep right there."

"Why should it be a channel?"

"To let that motorboat get into shore—or the rowboat. They'd run aground otherwise. Give me the light. I'll bet we've found where that boat was hidden."

He played the flashlight on the surface of the water and then they could see clearly that the bottom of the cove was broken by a deep channel at that point, several feet in width, leading directly toward a clump of bushes at the shore.

Keeping well to the side of the channel and in the shallow water, the Hardy boys made their way over to the bushes.

Then, when the beam of the flashlight was cast on the dense covert of branches, the mystery was clear.

Beyond the bushes was a dark opening in the rock

"A cave!" exclaimed Frank, in a suppressed tone.

It was so cleverly concealed that it could not have been seen in the clear light of the day except at close quarters. The glare of the flashlight, however, cast the dark opening into prominence behind the screen of leaves.

This, then, was the explanation of the boat's disappearance. There was a channel in the cove enabling the smugglers to row the boat directly into this cave in the rock. This also probably explained the presence of the motorboat.

"They went in here," said Joe.

"We'll explore it."

Having gone so far, there was no going back. The boys were fully determined to keep on the track of the smugglers. They did not know what lay behind the darkness of that silent and mysterious opening in the rock. But they meant to find out, no matter what the risks.

Cautiously, they advanced into the bushes, which gave way protestingly before them. The branches whipped their faces. The water was still shallow, for there was a narrow ledge along the side of the channel and, moreover, it was now low tide.

At last the bushes closed behind them. The Hardy boys were standing in the entrance to a secret passage, pressed close against the rocky wall of the cave.

CHAPTER XVII

THE CHAMBER IN THE CLIFF

Frank switched on the flashlight.

The beam illuminated the depths of the dark passage. Far ahead of the brothers they glimpsed a grey shape just above the surface of the glistening water.

For a moment they were startled, then they recognized that the grey shape was nothing more than the rowboat that had passed by them in the darkness outside the cove. It had been drawn up close to a natural wharf hewn out of the solid rock. It swayed to and fro with the motion of the water.

The boys made their way forward along the ledge, which was wide enough for one person to walk on, until at last the ledge widened out and proved to be a path leading to the wharf.

There was not a sound in the passage but the drip-drip of water from the gloomy walls.

The Hardy boys stole quietly forward along the wharf, passed the boat, and then looked about them.

Frank played the beam of the flashlight all about the place until at last the glare revealed a dark opening immediately ahead.

It was a crude arch in the rock and beyond it he could see a steep flight of wooden steps.

His heart was pounding with excitement. There was no doubt now that they had discovered the smugglers' secret.

"We've found it," he whispered to Joe. "We've found the passage. This must be directly underneath the house on the cliff."

"We'll have to go quietly."

The light cast strange shadows through the gloomy passage in the rocks. Water dripped from the walls. Water dripped from their clothing. They tiptoed quietly forward beneath the archway until they reached the flight of steps.

Then, quietly, almost stealthily, they began to ascend.

The place was in a deathlike silence. It was as if they were in a tomb. So quiet was the strange stairway in the cliff that the boys could hardly believe that men had been there but a short while before.

Step by step they ascended the stairs, and at last Frank's flashlight showed that they were approaching a door. It was set directly in a frame in the wall of rock at which the stairs ended. The passageway curved above them in a rocky ceiling.

They stood on the steps outside the door.

Should they enter?

They did not know what lay beyond. They might be entering the very haunt of the smugglers. In fact, this was most probable. And in that event they would not have a chance of escape.

For a while they remained there, not knowing whether to

retreat or go on.

Then Frank stepped forward. He pressed his ear against the door and listened intently.

There was not a sound.

He peered around the sides of the door to see if he could catch a glimpse of light. There was only darkness. At length he decided that there was no one immediately beyond the door and he made up his mind to go ahead.

He whispered his decision to Joe, who nodded.

"I'm with you."

The door was opened by a latch, and Frank tried it cautiously. At first it was obstinate.

Then, with an abrupt clatter that echoed from wall to wall and seemed to the ears of the boys to create a hideous and deafening uproar, the latch snapped and the door swung open.

They did not immediately cross the threshold. Perhaps their approach had been heard. Perhaps the smugglers lay in wait for them beyond. So they remained there in silence for several minutes, listening for the slightest sound.

However, it became apparent that the dark chamber was empty, so Frank switched on the flashlight.

The vivid beam cut the darkness and revealed a gloomy cave in the very center of the cliff, hewn out of the rock. It had been a natural cave, just as the tunnel in the cliff had been a natural passageway, but the roof had been bolstered up by great beams and the sides had been chipped away while the floor had been leveled. It was a secret chamber in the heart of the rock.

The light revealed the fact that this chamber was used as a storeroom, for there were huge boxes, bales and packages distributed about the floor and piled against the walls.

"Smuggled goods!" exclaimed Frank.

His suspicions seemed verified by the fact that the majority of the boxes bore labels of foreign countries. Chinese characters were scribbled across them in practically every case.

Seeing that the chamber was unoccupied, the boys stepped through the doorway and looked about them. The flashlight illuminated the murky corners of the cave.

"This must be where they store all the stuff," Joe said, as he inspected one of the boxes.

"There must be another opening that leads to the top of the cliff. They probably bring the stuff up to the house and then dispose of it from there."

"You'd think they would keep it at the Polucca place instead of down here."

"Probably they are afraid the house might be raided at some time or another. That's why they keep the goods hidden in this place. It would be mighty hard for any one to find it here."

"But how do they get the stuff out of here? There's no doorway that I can see."

The light of the flashlight played upon the walls.

No doorway, no opening of any kind, was revealed.

"That's strange," said Frank. "There must be some way out."

They began to move about the chamber. Across some of the bales of goods had been thrown rich bolts of silk, while valuable tapestries were also lying carelessly on the floor. In one corner were three or four boxes piled on top of one another. Frank accidentally knocked the flashlight against one of these and it gave forth a hollow sound.

"It's empty," he said.

An idea struck him that perhaps these boxes had been piled up to conceal some passage leading out of the secret chamber. He mentioned his suspicion to Joe.

"But how could they pile the boxes up there after they went out?" his brother questioned.

"This gang are smart enough for anything. Let's move these boxes away."

He seized the topmost box. It was very light and he removed it from the top of the pile without difficulty.

"I thought so!" exclaimed Frank, with satisfaction.

For the light revealed the top of a door which had hitherto been hidden from view.

The boys lost no time in moving the rest of the boxes, and the entire door was soon in sight. Then the boys discovered how it was possible for the boxes to be piled up in such a position in spite of the fact that the smugglers had left the chamber and closed the door behind them.

Attached to the bottom of the door was a small wooden platform that projected out some distance over the floor of the cave and on this platform the boxes had been piled.

"They are kept there all the time, as a blind," he said. "Whenever any one leaves the cave and closes the door the boxes swing in with the platform and it looks as though they were piled up on the floor."

The ingenuity of the contrivance won their reluctant admiration.

"What shall we do?" asked Joe, looking through the doorway into the darkness beyond. "Go ahead?"

"We've come this far, and there's no sense in turning back. Let's go."

Frank stepped on into the passage beyond. He had hardly

switched on the flashlight, revealing a crude flight of stairs that led from the rocky landing, before he stiffened and laid a warning hand on his brother's arm.

"Voices!" he whispered.

They listened.

They heard a man's voice in the distance. They could not distinguish what he was saying, for he was still too far away, but gradually the tones grew louder. Then, to their alarm, they heard footsteps.

Hastily, they retreated into the secret chamber.

"Quick! The door," snapped Frank.

They closed the door quietly.

"Now the boxes. If they come in here they'll notice that the boxes have been moved. Quick."

Swiftly the Hardy boys began to pile the empty boxes back on the platform that projected from the bottom of the door. They worked as quietly as possible and as they worked they heard the footsteps on the stairs drawing closer and closer.

Finally, the topmost box was in place.

"Out the other door."

They sped across the floor of the chamber toward the door that led to the stairs they had just recently ascended, but hardly had they reached it before they heard a rattle at the latch of the door on the opposite side of the cave.

"We haven't time," whispered Frank. "Hide."

The beam of the flashlight revealed a number of boxes close by the door. Over these boxes had been thrown a heavy bolt of silk, the folds of which hung down to the floor. They scrambled swiftly in behind the boxes, pressing themselves close against the wall. They did not have more than time to hide themselves and switch out the light before they heard the other door open.

"There's a package of dope in that shipment that came in last night," they heard a husky voice saying. "We'll bring it upstairs, for Burke says he can get rid of it for us right away. No use leaving it down here."

"Right," they heard some one else reply. "Anything else to go up?"

"No. We won't start moving the rest of this until the end of the week. It's too dangerous. Let Burke take out the shipment he has, along with this dope, and then we'll lay low for a few days. I'm getting a bit nervous."

"What does the big boss think about it?"

"That's his idea too. Here—wait till I switch on that light."

There was a click, and suddenly the chamber was flooded with light. The cave had been wired for electricity.

The Hardy boys crouched in their hiding place. Their hearts were pounding madly.

Would they be discovered?

Footsteps slowly approached the boxes behind which they were concealed!

CHAPTER XVIII

A STARTLING DISCOVERY

The Hardy boys were tense with a realization of their peril.

The strong electric light that hung from the center of the ceiling cast such a vivid illumination that they were sure they would be seen, particularly when they found that the boxes behind which they were hidden were spaced some distance apart. But for the folds of silk that hung down over the opening they would certainly have been seen.

"Here's some of that special silk," they heard the first man say. "Perhaps I'd better bring it up too. Burke was saying he could handle some more silk."

"We're done for!" thought Frank. "If he ever comes close enough to pick up that silk he'll see us, sure."

But the other man objected.

"What's the use? You won't get any more thanks for carrying all that stuff upstairs, even if Burke does take it. And if he doesn't, you'll just have to cart it all the way down again. My motto in this gang is to do just what Snackley tells me and no

117

more."

"I guess you're right. We'll just bring up the dope."

To the relief of the boys the man turned away and went back to the other side of the chamber. They could hear a rustling sound. Then came the words:

"Well, we've got it. Let's go back up."

The switch snapped and the cavern was steeped in darkness immediately. It was a darkness immeasurably welcome to the lads crouched behind the boxes. They began to breathe more easily. They heard the door close and then they could hear the footsteps of the two men as they ascended the stairs in the passageway.

When the footsteps could be heard no more, Frank switched on the flashlight with a sigh of relief.

"That was a close call. Gosh, but I was sure they had us."

"We wouldn't have had any chance with that pair. You can bet your life they carry guns."

"Well, let's follow them."

"I'm with you. We know we're on the right track."

"And we know we're liable to blunder right into the whole den of smugglers if we don't watch our step. It's going to be ticklish from now on."

"It can't be any more ticklish than it has been. I lived about ten years while that pair was in here."

They crossed the chamber and again opened the door. Cautiously, they stepped out on the landing, closed the door behind them, and again confronted the flight of steps.

"I'll go first," said Frank. "Stick close behind me."

He decided to turn out the flashlight, because it was barely possible that the smugglers might have a guard at the top of the stairs, in which event their approach would be discovered. So, in the inky blackness, they ascended, step after step.

They reached the top of the first flight of stairs and then they found themselves upon a crude landing of planks which ran along the side of the rock wall for some distance until it ended in another flight of steps.

Here the boys stopped again to listen. All was as silent as the tomb save for the distant pounding of the sea upon the cliff.

"I don't hear a sound," whispered Joe,

"Come on," came from his brother.

The passage through the rock was of considerable depth, and they went on up countless steps until their limbs were weary. They had never realized that the cliff was so high until now.

But at length they reached the final landing and there they were confronted by another door. This door, they assumed, either led out into the open or into some cave just below the surface of the ground. Perhaps, thought Frank, it even led into the cellar of the Polucca house.

The boys pressed close to the door, taking care to make no noise, and listened.

They heard not a sound.

Still, with the caution arising from their previous narrow escape, they decided to wait a little while longer. As later events proved, it was well that they did.

For a while they could hear nothing from beyond the door and there was no indication that any one was there. But, after listening intently for as long as five minutes, they heard a queer shuffling sound and then a sigh. That was all.

"Some one there!" breathed Frank, in a low whisper.

Joe nodded in the darkness.

They did not know what to do. It seemed apparent that there was some one beyond the door. Possibly a sentry. If there was only one man it might be possible to attack him and disarm him, although it was scarcely possible that they could do this without noise and without attracting the attention of the smugglers.

The problem was solved for them.

A door thudded in the distance. Then there was a muffled murmur of voices, growing in volume, and a trampling of feet.

"I tell you this nonsense has gone far enough. He'll sign, and he'll sign right now, or I'll know the reason why."

The boys started. For the voice was none other than the voice of the man who had ordered them out of the cove that afternoon.

"That's the stuff, chief!" returned some one. "Make him sign and promise to keep his mouth shut."

"If he doesn't he'll never live to tell about it, that's one thing sure!" snapped the first man coldly.

There was the sound of a switch being snapped, and then the boys could see a yellow beam of light beneath the door at their feet. From the sounds they judged that three or four men had entered the room beyond.

"Well, he's still here," said the man who had been addressed as "chief." He strode across the room and the boys could hear a chair scrape on the board floor. "You'll find that this is an easier place to get into than it is to get out of."

A weary voice answered him. The tones were low. The boys could not make out the words.

"You're a prisoner here and you'll be a prisoner here until you die unless you sign that paper."

Again the weary voice spoke, but, as before, the tones were

so low that the words were indistinguishable.

"You won't sign, eh? We'll see about that!"

"Wait till he goes hungry for a few days and then he'll think differently," put in one of the other men. There was a hoarse laugh from his companions.

"Yes, you'll be hungry enough before we're through with you. I can promise you that," said the harsh voice. "Are you going to sign?"

"No," they heard the prisoner in the other room answer.

Who was this man who was evidently held captive by the smugglers in the underground room? The same thought was in the mind of each boy as he listened to the conversation.

"You know too much about us. You've found out too much, and we'll never let you get out of here to use your information. You may as well get that straight. You've read that paper. If you don't sign it you will starve."

The prisoner evidently did not reply.

"Give him a taste of the hot iron," suggested one of the smugglers.

"No, nothing like that. It's too crude. I'm giving him his chance. He can sign this paper now or take the consequences."

Still there was no reply.

"Getting obstinate, are you? Won't you even answer me!" The leader of the gang was evidently getting angry. Suddenly he shouted out:

"Sign this paper, Hardy, or you'll starve—as sure as my name is Snackley!"

CHAPTER XIX

CAPTURED

The worst fears of the Hardy boys were realized.

They had been unable to distinguish clearly the voice of the prisoner until then, for it had been muffled by the intervening door, but all along they had suspected that it was their father. Now they knew, and they knew also that he was a captive of Snackley, the head of the gang of smugglers.

Joe gave a perceptible start, but Frank laid a warning hand upon his brother's arm. Now, of all times, there was need for caution.

They listened.

"I won't sign it," replied Fenton Hardy clearly.

Snackley replied:

"You heard what I said. Sign or starve."

"I'll starve."

"You'll think differently in a day or so. You're pretty hungry now, Hardy, but you'll be a lot hungrier later on. And thirsty, too. You'll be ready to sell your soul for a drop of water or a bite to eat."

"I won't sign."

"After all, we're not asking very much. You've discovered a number of things that we want you to forget about. It won't hurt you to go back to Bayport and say that you couldn't find out anything about us. Nobody knows where you have been."

"I've found out all I wanted to know about you, Snackley. I've got enough evidence to send you to the penitentiary for the rest of your life. And I have more than that."

"What do you mean—more than that?"

"I know enough to have you sent to the electric chair."

There was a sudden commotion in the room and two or three of the smugglers began talking at once.

"You're crazy!" shouted Snackley, but there was a current of uneasiness in his voice. "You're crazy. You don't know anything about me."

"I know enough to have you sent up for murder."

"All the more reason why you're not going to get out of here without signing this paper. You can count yourself lucky you have even this chance of getting out alive. By all rights we should knock you on the head and heave you over the cliff into the sea."

"I won't sign."

"Don't be foolish. All we ask you to do is to agree that you won't make use of the information you have. I admit that you've stumbled on some of our secrets, and we can't afford to turn you loose and have the federal agents about our ears in no time."

"You must trust me very much. What is to prevent me from

signing that paper and then going back on my word?" asked Fenton Hardy curiously.

"We know you too well, Hardy. We know that if you signed that promise you would keep it."

"Exactly. And that is why I won't sign it. I wouldn't be doing my duty if I agreed to any scheme that would protect you."

"How about your family? Are you doing your duty to them by being so obstinate?"

There was silence for a while. Then Fenton Hardy answered slowly:

"They would rather know that I died doing my duty than have me come back to them as a protector of smugglers and criminals."

"You have a very high sense of duty," sneered Snackley. "But perhaps you'll think better of it after a while. Are you thirsty?"

There was no reply.

"Are you hungry?"

Still no answer.

"You know you are. And you'll be hungrier and thirstier before we are through with you. We'll put food and water in your sight but you won't be able to reach it. You'll die of thirst and starvation—unless you sign that paper."

"I'll never sign it."

"All right. Come on, men. We'll leave him to himself and give him time to think about it."

Footsteps resounded as Snackley and the others began to leave the room, and finally they died away and a door banged.

Fenton Hardy was left alone.

Joe made a sudden move toward the door, but Frank restrained him.

"Not just yet," he cautioned. "They may have left some one to guard him."

So the boys waited, listening intently at the door.

But there were no further sounds from within the room. At length, satisfied that his father had indeed been left alone, Frank fumbled for the latch of the door.

Noiselessly, he managed to open it. He pressed in on the door until it was open about an inch, then he peeped through the aperture.

He found himself on the threshold of a sort of cellar, a damp and mouldy chamber, of about the same size as the storage room in the heart of the cliff, with the difference that whereas the first room was a cave in the rock, this place had been dug out of the earth. It was floored with planks and a lone electric light cast a yellowish illumination over the scene. There was a crude table and a few chairs, while in one corner stood a small camp-bed.

On this bed he spied his father.

Fenton Hardy was bound hand and foot to the cot, so tightly trussed up that he was unable to move more than a few inches in any direction. He was lying flat on his back, staring up at the muddy ceiling of his prison. On a chair beside the cot was a large sheet of paper, presumably the document the smugglers were asking him to sign.

The detective did not hear the door open. As Frank looked at him he was conscious of a change in the appearance of his father, a change that shocked him extremely. For Fenton Hardy was thin and pale, his cheeks were sunken and he looked like a man who was famished for want of food.

Frank opened the door a little wider and tiptoed into the room. Joe followed quietly.

They knew that there was danger of the smugglers returning at any moment. They knew that they must work swiftly and quietly if they were to effect the release of their father.

A slight sound attracted Fenton Hardy's attention and he slowly turned his head. When his gaze rested on the figures of the two boys who were stealing across the floor toward him he almost uttered an exclamation of amazement but he managed to check the involuntary utterance, although his face lighted up with relief.

Quickly, the Hardy boys reached his bedside. Frank drew out his pocketknife and, without a word, without even a whisper, began to hack at the ropes that bound his father. But the knife was dull and the ropes were heavy.

Joe had lost his knife in the water soon after they had left Bayport, and although he searched about the room, he was unable to find one, so he set himself to the laborious business of trying to untie the knots.

Every moment was precious. At any second, the boys knew, they might hear the footsteps of the approaching smugglers. They worked with frantic caution, working against time.

Frank hacked at the ropes, but the dull blade seemed to make little progress. Joe fumbled at the obstinate knots until his fingernails were broken, but he could scarcely loosen the strands.

Minutes passed—slowly and agonizingly. Fenton Hardy could give no assistance. He had to lie there in silence, not daring even to encourage the lads by a whisper. The silence was broken only by the heavy breathing of the two boys, by the scarcely audible sound of the knife against the ropes.

At last the knife cut through one of the ropes and Fenton Hardy's feet were free. Frank pulled the ropes away, but a loose end fell on the floor with a light sound.

Slight as the noise was, it seemed to them almost deafening.

in view of the necessity for silence. Desperately, Frank prepared to set to work to cut through the ropes that bound Fenton Hardy's arms. And, even as he reached over with the knife, they heard a sound that sent a thrill of terror through them.

It was a heavy footstep beyond the door through which the smugglers had recently disappeared!

Some one was approaching the underground room.

Frank strained at the knife, but the ropes were stubborn. The dull blade made little impression at first. But at last the rope began to give, and finally, as Fenton Hardy gave a mighty effort, it snapped, and the detective was free.

But the footsteps on the stairs had drawn nearer and it was followed by others. The smugglers were returning.

"Quick!" whispered Frank, as he flung the ropes aside.

"I—I can't—hurry!" gasped out Fenton Hardy. "I've been here too—too long." He could hardly utter the words. His face showed his exhaustion.

"But we've got to hurry, dad!" came excitedly from Frank. "See if you can't make it."

"I'll—I'll do my—my best," returned his father.

"If those fellows come back let's fight for it," put in Joe desperately.

"You bet we'll fight," answered Frank in a voice that meant a great deal.

Fenton Hardy got to his feet as hastily as he could, but when he stood up on the floor he reeled and would have fallen had not Joe grasped his arm. He had been lying bound to the cot for so long and he was so weak from hunger that a fit of dizziness had attacked him. It soon passed, however, and the three hastened toward the door through which the Hardy boys had entered.

But the smugglers were very close now. The Hardys could hear the coarse voices just outside the other door.

There was no chance of escape.

Just as the Hardy boys and their father crossed the threshold the door on the opposite side of the room was flung open.

Frank had a confused glimpse of the dark man, Snackley, whom they had seen in the cove that afternoon, with half a dozen rough men crowding behind him. Then he saw Snackley whip a revolver from his pocket.

The chief of the smugglers was filled with astonishment, but he did not lose his presence of mind. The weapon was leveled at Frank before he had time to close the door.

Snackley did not speak. He pressed the trigger and the revolver roared, the echoes crowding on one another in that narrow space. The bullet chipped into the wood of the door.

Frank ducked. Joe, who was in the lead, flung himself to one side. Fenton Hardy stumbled out on to the landing at the top of the stairs.

"Come back!" roared Snackley, plunging across the room. "Come back or I'll fire again!"

As the smuggler drew closer Frank crouched for a spring, and then leaped directly at Snackley. He struck out at the man's wrist and the revolver flew out of the rascal's grasp, skidding across the floor into a corner.

Then they grappled, and so sudden had been Frank's attack that the smuggler was taken by surprise and he reeled up against the wall. But his companions rushed to his rescue. Frank was swiftly overpowered and dragged away, while other smugglers, with drawn revolvers, pursued Joe and Fenton Hardy out on to the landing. Being unarmed, they were forced to submit, otherwise they would have been shot without mercy.

The struggle was short. The menacing revolvers gave the smugglers the upper hand.

Within five minutes Fenton Hardy was bound to the cot again while the Hardy boys were seated, trussed up and unable to move, on two chairs near by. They were captives of the smugglers!

CHAPTER XX

DIRE THREATS

Snackley, once he had recovered from his first consternation and surprise, was in high humor.

"Just in time!" he chuckled, rubbing his hands with satisfaction. "Just in time! If we'd been a few minutes later they'd have been away from us altogether."

The Hardy boys were silent. They were sick with disappointment. It had seemed that escape was certain, and then, in a twinkling, the tables had been turned and now they were all worse off than they had been before.

"What will we do with 'em, chief?" asked one of the men.

The voice sounded familiar to the boys and they looked up. Not altogether to their surprise, they saw that the fellow was none other than Redhead, whom they had seen at the Polucca place the day Frank discovered his father's cap.

"Do with them?" exclaimed Snackley. "That's quite a problem. We have three on our hands now, where we had only one. We have to make three people keep their mouths shut instead of only one. We have three people to keep guard over now."

"We ought to do what I wanted to do in the first place," declared Redhead doggedly. "As long as Hardy is alive, he's dangerous."

"You mean we should get rid of him?"

"Sure, we ought to get rid of him—and get rid of those boys of his, too."

"That's easier said than done," returned Snackley, but with a sinister look at the man on the cot.

"I should think you had enough on your conscience already, Snackley!" exclaimed Fenton Hardy. "But I suppose you're hardened enough for anything," he added bitterly. He was thinking more of his sons and their possible fate than of himself.

"Don't you bother about my conscience," sneered Snackley; but a shadow crossed his face. "What do you know about me, anyhow?" he demanded roughly.

"I know all about what happened to Felix Polucca. He had a big treasure hidden in that house on the cliff and you got it, and then you started to use the place for your smuggling operations."

"O, shut up!" Snackley snapped. "I'm going to fix you, and those kids of yours, too! Just wait and see!"

Four of the smugglers had been whispering among themselves at the back of the room during this talk between the chief smuggler and the detective, and now one of these men stepped forward.

"Got a word to say to you, chief," he began, addressing Snackley.

"What is it now?" The chief smuggler's voice was surly.

"It's about what's to be done with these three, now we have 'em prisoners," returned the man hesitatingly. "Of course, your business is your own and we're not asking any questions about what happened to Felix Polucca, but we're in this game of smuggling, see? We don't stand for anything that's too red-handed."

"That's the truth!" put in another of the men.

"Kind of chicken-hearted," sneered Snackley. "You look out or I'll fire the lot of you!"

"No, you won't, chief," replied the first man who had addressed him. "We've helped in this smuggling, and we're going to have our full share of what's coming to us."

"We've got another plan about those three prisoners," put in a fellow who had not yet spoken. "I think it would work out grand."

"What plan?" questioned the chief smuggler briefly.

"We've been talking about Li Chang."

"What about him?"

"Turn 'em over to Li Chang. He's sailing back to China in the morning. Have 'em put on board his ship."

Snackley scratched his head for a moment. Evidently the idea caught his fancy.

"Not bad," he muttered. "I hadn't thought of Li Chang. Yes, he'd be able to look after them. He'd see to it that they never returned," and he grinned grimly.

"He'd probably dump 'em overboard before they got to China at all," declared Redhead smugly. "Li Chang doesn't like to feed passengers if they can be got rid of."

"So much the better. We won't be responsible."

"Leave it to Li Chang. The old villain would just like to have three white men in his power. He'll attend to them."

Snackley reached over and picked up the document from the floor, where it had fallen in the struggle. He glanced at it and then tore it into pieces.

"We won't need this. You've lost your chance, Hardy. If you had signed it you would have been free by now. But you'll never be free—not with three of you knowing our secret. It's too risky. You'll all be turned over to Li Chang. He brought in a little cargo this week and his ship is to sail in the morning. You will go with him."

Fenton Hardy was silent. He had resolved not to plead for his own safety.

"Well," said Snackley, "haven't you anything to say?"

"Nothing. Do as you wish with me. But let the boys go."

"We'll stick with you, dad," said Frank quickly.

"We sure will!" added Joe.

"You certainly will," declared Snackley. "I'm not going to let one of you have the chance of getting back to Bayport with your story."

The chief of the smugglers stood in the center of the room for a while, contemplating his captives with a bitter smile. Then he turned suddenly on his heel.

"Well, they're safe enough," he said to Redhead. "We have that business with Burke to attend to. You two," he said, speaking to two of his men, "had better go down to the cove and take the rowboat out. Signal to Li Chang that we need the motorboat sent in at once. The rest of you come and help load Burke's truck. If any nosey policeman came along and found it in the lane we'd be done for."

"How about them?" asked Redhead, indicating the prisoners.

"They're safe enough. But I guess we'd better leave one guard, anyway. Malloy, you stay here and keep watch."

Malloy, a surly and truculent fellow in overalls and a ragged sweater, nodded and sat down on a box near the door. This arrangement seemed to satisfy Snackley, and after warning Malloy not to fall asleep on the job and to see to it that the prisoners did not escape, he left the room, followed by Redhead and the other smugglers, with the exception of two who left by the other door. Their footsteps could be heard as they went down the flight of stairs leading to the bottom of the cliff.

A heavy silence fell over the room after the departure of the smugglers. Malloy crouched gloomily on the box, gazing blankly at the floor. The butt of a revolver projected from his hip pocket.

Frank strained against the ropes that bound him to the chair. But the smugglers had done their task well. He could scarcely budge.

"We're done for, I guess," he heard Joe say.

Frank seldom gave up heart, but this time he could see no ray of hope.

"I'm afraid so. Looks as if we'd be with Li Chang by morning."

"But we don't want to go to China, Frank!"

"We may never get to China, Joe. Didn't you hear what they said? For all we know, that rascally Chinaman, whoever he is, may heave us overboard when he gets well out in the ocean."

"You fellows shut up," growled Malloy. "Shut up, I tell you, or I'll make it hot for you," and he tapped his revolver suggestively.

After that an ominous silence fell between the prisoners. Frank and Joe were downhearted. It looked as if their fate were sealed.

CHAPTER XXI

QUICK WORK

The Hardy boys glanced over at their father on the cot.

To their surprise they saw that he was smiling. Frank was on the point of asking him what he found in the situation to smile at when he caught a warning glance. He looked over at the guard.

Malloy was not bothering with the prisoners. He was not even looking in their direction. Instead, his head was already beginning to nod, as though he were going to sleep.

Snackley had made a poor selection when he chose Malloy as guard. The man had been up the entire previous night helping bring in the shipment of smuggled goods from Li Chang's vessel, and he had had no sleep that day. He was very tired. Sleep stole upon him without his being aware of it.

Several times he straightened up and rubbed his eyes, but eventually he would bow his head again and give in to the luxury of a little doze.

In the meantime, Mr. Hardy was busy. He had profited by

his previous experience.

When the smugglers seized him and attempted to tie him to the bed for the second time he had made use of a trick frequently employed by magicians and professional "escape" artists, who guarantee to escape from ropes and strait-jackets. He had expanded his chest and held his muscles rigid, keeping his arms as far away from his sides as possible, so that later, when he relaxed, he found that the ropes did not bind him as tightly as his captors had intended.

This gave him a small leeway. He found that the ropes were especially slack about his right wrist, so he began to work laboriously to free himself. For a long time he thought it would be impossible, and the rope chafed his wrist, but at last he managed to slide his hand free.

Joe and Frank watched this performance with amazement, and new hope came into their eyes as they saw their father slowly groping for one of the knots. The detective fumbled at it for a while. It was slow work, for he had but one hand free, but in their haste the smugglers had not tied the knot as firmly as they should, and before long Fenton Hardy had loosened it to such an extent that soon the ends of the rope fell away.

His arms were now free, so he braced himself against the sides of the bed and struggled to release his feet. They had not been bound so securely, being simply tied down under one strand of rope about the cot, and after silently struggling for a few minutes he was able to work his way free.

The detective's next move was to take off his boots, which he did swiftly and quietly, placing them noiselessly on the bed. Then he crept out onto the floor and began to steal over toward the guard.

Malloy was half asleep, but the detective had not gone more than two yards before a slight sound, a slight creaking of the floor, warned the guard that something was amiss.

He turned, blinking.

A look of intense amazement crossed Malloy's face and he opened his mouth to yell for help, but Fenton Hardy leaped across the intervening space and hurled himself upon the smuggler before the guard had time to utter more than a muffled gasp.

He clapped one hand over Malloy's mouth and bore the guard to the floor, where they rolled over and over in a desperate and silent struggle. Although Fenton Hardy was weakened by his imprisonment and privation and although the smuggler was strong and wiry, the detective had the advantage of a surprise attack, and Malloy had no time to collect his faculties.

Joe and Frank watched the battle in an agony of suspense. It was, they knew, their last hope.

Fenton Hardy still kept his hand over the other man's mouth, although Malloy was gasping and gurgling and making frantic efforts to call out for help. The detective dug his knee into Malloy's stomach and when the smuggler tried to wriggle out of the way he snatched for the revolver.

Their hands closed about the butt of the weapon at the same instant.

The struggle was short and bitter.

Malloy tugged at the revolver, trying to draw it from his pocket. Fenton Hardy dug his knee sharply against the man and Malloy loosened his grasp, with a groan of pain. The detective snatched the revolver free and then flung himself back, leveling the weapon at Malloy.

"Not a word out of you!" he whispered.

Malloy's hands rose in the air. He did not utter a sound. He was sitting helplessly on the floor, his mouth opening and closing as he painfully drew breath. He was beaten.

The detective spied a knife in a leather sheath at the smuggler's belt so he reached forward and seized the weapon.

Then, still keeping Malloy covered with the revolver, he walked slowly backward until he reached Joe's side. Without removing his eyes from the smuggler, Fenton Hardy bent down and sliced at the ropes that bound his son.

The knife was sharp and the ropes soon fell apart. Joe leaped from the chair, casting aside the rope ends, and took the proffered knife. Then, while his father still covered Malloy, he went over to Frank and set him free.

Still without saying a word, Fenton Hardy motioned toward the bed and indicated by signs that the smuggler was to lie down on the cot. A gesture of refusal on the part of Malloy was met by a vigorous forward thrust of the revolver and the smuggler hastily retreated.

The ropes on the bed had not been cut, so they were still available for trussing up Malloy just as Mr. Hardy had been bound. The boys did the job with neatness and despatch and they even gagged the smuggler with his own handkerchief and one of the ropes from the chairs.

Within five minutes their erstwhile guard was lying helpless on the bed, bound hand and foot and gagged so firmly that only a muffled and subdued muttering escaped him.

"What now?" asked Frank, in a low tone.

"We can't go out by the cove," replied his father. "There are two men down there now signaling to the motorboat. We'd better go upstairs."

"Where does that lead to?"

"Outside. It will bring us into the shed near the house."

Fenton Hardy moved over toward the door.

"We haven't any time to lose," he said. "I have the revolver

If we meet any one—"

He opened the door cautiously and peeped out. There was no one beyond. There was nothing but a flight of steps leading upward into darkness.

The detective went forward, his sons following close at his heels.

Step by step they made their way on up in the darkness, for Joe had closed the door behind them and Frank did not dare make use of the flashlight.

At last Fenton Hardy came to a stop. He was fumbling at something immediately above.

Then the boys saw a faint opening which grew larger above them and resolved itself into a square of grey light against which the head and shoulders of their father were fully silhouetted. Fenton Hardy had raised the trapdoor that concealed the entrance to the underground caves and passages.

Mr. Hardy looked out carefully. There was no sign of the smugglers. He proceeded to the very top of the steps, then moved clear of the stairway.

Frank and Joe followed, rising out of the ground like mysterious spirits of the earth, and the three stood in the shelter of the shed.

It was a dark night and the trees were moaning in the wind from the sea. Immediately before them rose the gloomy mass of the house on the cliff. There were no lights.

In the direction of the lane they could hear dull sounds, no doubt from the truck that the smugglers were loading with goods which were to be disposed of by the man called Burke.

"Safe so far," whispered the detective to his sons.

They moved out of the shed, after closing the trapdoor, and stood in the shadows.

"We can't go by way of the lane," whispered Frank.

"There's a prisoner in the cellar of that house," said Fenton Hardy. "I hate to go without setting him free."

"A prisoner?"

"I heard them talking about him."

"Why can't we go to town for help?"

"Once they find us gone they'll clear out."

"But three of us can't do much against this gang. They'll just capture us all again."

The detective considered this for a moment. At last he sighed.

"Yes, the risk is too great!" he said. "And I've let you take too many risks already. We'd better go back to town."

Having arrived at this decision, they moved slowly across the grass of the yard, heading toward the bushes that flanked the lane. The great bulk of the old stone house loomed heavily and darkly in the night.

Then, suddenly, they heard a harsh sound that struck terror into their hearts—the clatter of the trapdoor being raised!

CHAPTER XXII

INTO THE HAUNTED HOUSE

A hoarse shout came through the darkness.

"Chief! Redhead! They've got away. Watch for 'em!"

Some one was scrambling through the opening in the shed, bellowing in a frantic voice, warning the other smugglers of the escape.

"Into the house!" snapped Fenton Hardy. He began to run swiftly across the yard toward the big gloomy house. Frank and Joe followed.

The man in the shed saw the moving figures.

The darkness was pierced by a flash of crimson and a revolver barked three times.

From the lane came sounds of running feet. A man was shouting:

"What is it? What's the matter?"

"They've got away! Hardy and them boys! They've escaped. Look! There they are now—running across the yard!"

The revolver spoke again. But the shots were wild, for the detective and his sons were soon lost to view in the shadows of the house.

With the uproar growing in volume behind them, they fled for the shelter of the building. It was their only refuge. If they attempted to escape to the road they would be almost certain of meeting some of the smugglers. They could not go back down the passageway. If they retreated they would be driven to the verge of the cliff.

Fenton Hardy sped around to the back door and flung it open. The fugitives raced into the kitchen and closed the door behind them.

Out of the darkness came a frightened voice.

"Who's there?"

It was so sudden and unexpected that their pulses leaped.

They made no answer.

"Who's there, I say? Is it you, Redhead?"

Still they did not reply. Fenton Hardy crept through the darkness in the direction of the voice.

"Speak! Quick! Speak, or I'll fire!"

The boys heard a sudden, scrambling sound. Their father had thrown himself upon the other man. The boys rushed in on the two struggling figures.

There was a deafening roar and a streak of flame. The man of the house had been armed with a shotgun, and in the struggle it had exploded.

Fortunately, the Hardy boys were not standing in the path of the shot. But the noise had attracted the attention of the smugglers outside the house, and in a few seconds the back door was flung open.

"They're in here!" some one yelled. "They're in the house!"

Fenton Hardy flung to one side the man with whom he had been struggling.

"Upstairs!" he called out to the two boys and ran on into the next room.

A feeble light was burning, a candle standing in its own grease near the bottom of the staircase. Up these stairs they fled, Joe pausing long enough to extinguish the candle. The room was plunged into darkness just as the first of the smugglers rushed through the doorway.

Fenton Hardy waited at the top of the stairs until the boys joined him.

Somebody in the room below lit a match.

The detective fired directly at the spluttering light. There was a muttered exclamation. The match was immediately extinguished by the smuggler who had been so incautious as to reveal his whereabouts in this manner. A whispered conversation followed.

"He's at the top of the stairs!" said one of the smugglers. "We can't rush him. He's got a revolver."

"Only one?"

"Yes. The kids aren't armed."

"Wait till he uses up his ammunition. Then we'll get him."

There was another whispered colloquy and then the smugglers apparently withdrew toward the doorway leading into the kitchen. Then, in a moment, a perfect fusillade of shots broke out.

But Fenton Hardy and the boys had withdrawn past the turn in the staircase and were well protected. They could hear the uproar of gunfire as the smugglers riddled the staircase with bullets.

"That should have finished 'em!" they could hear Snackley

saying. "If they're on the stairs at all they're as dead as mutton by now."

"Best be careful," muttered one of the men. "Hardy has a gun."

"Where did he get it?"

"From the guard. They tied him up."

"Lucky they didn't get away altogether. Wait till I talk to Malloy!"

"He was tied fast to the bed when we came back up the stairs. They had taken his gun and gagged him. He said they had just gone, so we made after them and came up through the trapdoor. They were just getting out of the shed when we saw 'em."

"What a fine chase we would have had if they had got out into the woods. Well, we have 'em trapped now."

Whispers followed. The boys listened. Once they heard some one say:

"The back stairs—"

Frank turned to his father.

"They're going to rush us by the back stairs!"

"I hadn't thought of that," said Mr. Hardy. "I wonder if there is any way of reaching the attic."

Frank took the flashlight from his pocket and switched it on. Just a few yards away he could distinguish a flight of stairs leading up to a trapdoor in the ceiling. At the same time he could hear a stealthy noise at the bottom of another flight of steps that led to the kitchen.

"Hurry!" he whispered, and the three moved silently down the hall until they reached the steps.

Joe went up first and Frank followed with the light, while

Fenton Hardy stood at the bottom of the steps to cover their retreat with the revolver.

When Joe reached the trapdoor he pushed at it. At first it proved stubborn and would not open. There was an anxious moment while he strove to force it open but in spite of all his efforts it would not budge.

"What's the matter?" asked Frank from below.

"It won't open."

Frank went on up the few remaining steps and added his efforts to those of his brother. Together they shoved at the trapdoor, and at last it moved, then opened, falling back with a loud crash.

There was a yell from the stairs.

"Hurry up, men! They're getting into the attic."

A rush of thudding footsteps followed as the smugglers raced up the steps. Joe scrambled through the opening and Frank followed. Fenton Hardy was only half way up the steps, however, when the first smugglers reached the hallway. The detective fired directly at them.

The smugglers who were in the lead fell back in a desperate attempt to reach cover, and in so doing they collided with those behind. For a few moments confusion prevailed, and Fenton Hardy took advantage of it to spring up the few remaining steps, scramble through the opening and fling the trapdoor back into place.

The Hardys found themselves in the inky darkness of the attic. Frank switched on the flashlight, and in its glare they saw that they were in a dusty chamber immediately below the roof. Old boxes and rubbish lay about.

"Where did they go?" they heard one of the smugglers ask.

"Into the attic," replied another. "Now we've got them where we want them."

"That's what you said last time."

"They can't get out of there. We've got them cornered."

Snackley's voice broke in.

"Hardy!" he shouted.

Mr. Hardy did not answer.

"Listen, Hardy!" went on Snackley. "We'll give you one minute to come down out of there."

Still no answer.

"The floors are thin, Hardy! We can fire right through 'em. You can't get out. We have you cornered. Better come down."

Frank flashed the light from side to side. It was evident that the smuggler spoke the truth. They were indeed cornered.

An interval of silence followed. Then came:

"Your last chance, Hardy!"

Frank flashed the light upon his father. Mr. Hardy was inspecting the chamber of the revolver. He held out the weapon with a gesture of despair. There were no more shells.

A shot sounded from below and a bullet ripped its way savagely through the flooring but a foot or so away from where the three sat. Another bullet tore through the wood of the trapdoor.

The Hardys sprang back and, making as little noise as possible, pressed themselves against the sloping walls of the attic, keeping as far away from the trapdoor as they could.

A few more shots resounded. The bullets were unpleasantly close.

Then Snackley spoke again.

"What do you think of it now, Hardy? Are you and your boys

ready to come down?"

They did not answer, for they knew that if they did their voices would reveal where they were standing and might bring a bullet. When they did not reply Snackley spoke to his men.

"Let 'em have a few more!"

An angry chorus of revolver shots followed. In the midst of the uproar some of the smugglers secured a long pole and pushed against the trapdoor with it. Before those above could avert the danger the trapdoor was flung wide open. It fell back with a crash.

A hand appeared through the trapdoor, holding a revolver, and then the head and shoulders of one of the smugglers followed. He peered into the darkness, holding the weapon in readiness. Some one had switched on a light in the hall so that the man's figure could be clearly seen.

"Come out of it!" he snapped, pointing the revolver directly at the dim figure of Frank. "Come out of it, or I'll shoot!"

Further resistance was useless.

With sinking heart Frank advanced toward the edge of the opening in the floor, while Joe and Fenton Hardy followed, with arms upraised. The smuggler backed his way down the steps, still keeping them covered, until he reached the bottom of the stairs.

The Hardys descended, conscious of an array of leveled revolvers that covered every movement. They saw Snackley standing in the forefront of the crowd. They were captured again.

CHAPTER XXIII

RESCUE

Snackley stepped forward.

"So!" he sneered. "You pretty nearly got away with it, didn't you?"

The captives did not answer. They were sick with disappointment. Just when escape had been within their grasp the smugglers had outwitted them.

"You bit off a little more than you could chew when you stacked up against me," bragged Snackley.

"What'll we do with 'em, chief?" asked one of the man.

"Take them back to the cave. We'll get them out to Li Chang right away. If they get away again there'll be trouble for you. Keep an eye on them."

"Shouldn't we tie them up?"

"There's no rope. It doesn't matter. Put a bullet through the first one that makes a false move. You hear that?" he said, turning to Fenton Hardy. "The first one that tries to escape

148

gets a bullet through him."

The three were surrounded by the smugglers. The light shone on their evil, bearded faces and glittered on the drawn revolvers. Fenton Hardy's useless weapon had been snatched from him.

"Downstairs!" snapped Snackley. "Get downstairs with you."

He prodded Frank with the barrel of his revolver as he spoke. The Hardy boys moved toward the stairs, their father in the rear. One of the smugglers went ahead in case the prisoners should by chance make some desperate break for freedom.

When they reached the lower room they paused while the man ahead lit a match. The electric light had been broken. Hardly had the match flared than there came the sound of thudding feet through the kitchen and the back door banged noisily.

Some one rushed into the room, gasping for breath. The light revealed him to be another of the smugglers.

"Police!" he exclaimed, in terror. "They're coming down the lane!"

A babel of voices followed. The smugglers came tumbling down the stairs in their haste. With one bound Snackley leaped forward and seized the man by the collar.

"What!" he exclaimed. "What's that you say? Police?"

"Down the lane!" gasped the man. "They came down the road in a car and they're closing in on the house. I saw them."

With a yell, Snackley flung the man to one side.

"Down into the cave!" he roared. "Quick!"

Confusion prevailed. In the resulting uproar the match went out and the room was plunged into darkness.

Frank resolved on a daring move. He was standing directly beside one of the smugglers, and as soon as the light went out he sprang at the fellow, dashing the revolver from his grasp. It clattered on the floor.

"Help!" roared the fellow, as they grappled together.

Fenton Hardy had also been watching for his chance, and he sprang through the darkness at Snackley. He collided heavily with the chief of the smugglers and they rolled on the floor in a desperate struggle.

It was impossible to distinguish friend from enemy in the darkness. Joe plunged into the midst of the surging figures and his fist smashed against the face of one of the smugglers, who gave a howl of pain.

Then, outside the house, another uproar burst forth.

Some one was banging on the front door. Men could be heard shouting to one another.

Snackley made a desperate effort and managed to get to his feet. He struck out with both fists and managed to break free from the detective. He whirled to one side, stumbled out into the kitchen, and then reached the back door. He flung the door open.

Almost instantly a dark figure appeared in the doorway. It was the figure of a man in the uniform of a state trooper with drawn revolver and Snackley shouted the warning to the smugglers in the other room.

"The police!" he roared. "Every man for himself! Make your getaway!"

The trooper shot through the doorway at him, but Snackley dodged to one side. There was a rush of footsteps from the other room as the rest of the smugglers raced out into the kitchen. The officers tried to hold them back, but they were too many for him and he was hurled against the wall.

Utter confusion prevailed. The place was in absolute darkness and out in the yard shots, shouts and hoarse imprecations mingled in an indescribable uproar.

One of the smugglers managed to reach the shed. He flung open the trapdoor and descended the steps. Some of his companions followed, and in the darkness and excitement their escape was unnoticed.

Half a dozen police officers were in the yard. They had been attracted to the house by the sound of the shots when the Hardys were pursued by the smugglers, and they had planned to surround the place. They would have succeeded in capturing the entire gang had it not been for the man on guard outside.

Back in the living room of the house Frank was still struggling with his antagonist. The man was strong and heavy, a rough-and-tumble fighter, and the boy soon found that he had his hands full. They struggled desperately in the darkness, the smuggler frantic with the fear of capture, Frank grimly resolved that the man should not get away.

Fenton Hardy headed toward the door leading into the kitchen. Just then a figure brushed by him. He made a grab for the man, but the fellow evaded him and raced toward the other side of the room.

The detective gave chase. The fugitive kicked open a door and ran toward the front of the house. Mr. Hardy could follow him quite easily by the sound of his footsteps.

The fugitive scurried into a front room and banged the door behind him. Mr. Hardy launched himself against the door, which had a lock that snapped when the door shut. For a moment he was balked. Then he stepped back a few paces and rushed at the door, plunging against it with his shoulder. The woodwork splintered. Another rush, and the door fell open. The detective reeled into the room.

His fugitive had disappeared.

But the room was faintly lighted, as there was a wide window, and in the gloom the detective could see a dark patch in the floor. It was a trapdoor leading evidently to the cellar.

He went down through the opening, finding a flight of stairs which he descended. He could hear footsteps receding through the darkness but he made his way across the uneven floor of the cellar.

The detective stopped and listened. He heard the hurrying footsteps as the smuggler went on to the far end of the cellar. Then, to his great surprise, he heard a voice. In the distance he saw a faint glow of light. Then he saw that the cellar was divided into two parts and that the fugitive had entered a small room.

He crept closer.

"What's happening?" he heard some one say in a weak voice.

"Everything," snarled a voice which he recognized as that of Snackley. The detective's heart leaped. "Everything is happening. The police are here."

"The police!"

"Yes—the police—state troopers, federal officers and all. But don't think you're going to have a chance of squealing on us. I'm going to fix you, as I should have done a long while ago."

The other voice rose, replete with terror.

"No! No! You won't do that, Snackley! Let me live!"

Fenton Hardy crept swiftly over to the door. He saw Snackley standing by a small cot in a cell-like room. On the cot crouched a haggard man whose hands were handcuffed behind him. His feet were shackled to one leg of the iron cot.

Snackley, with a grim look of cruelty on his face, was raising a heavy club he had picked up.

There was no time to lose. The detective sprang through the doorway.

He plunged at Snackley just as the smuggler raised the club to strike.

Snackley reeled against the wall, with Fenton Hardy at his throat. Desperately, the smuggler tried to raise the weapon, but the detective had seized his wrist. They swayed to and fro, stumbling about on the muddy floor. Mr. Hardy had the advantage in that he had taken Snackley by surprise. He pinned the smuggler against the wall, twisting his wrist. The club fell to the floor.

Snackley plunged forward and they lost their footing, rolling about in the mud. Suddenly, Fenton Hardy wrenched his arm free, sprawled over and managed to seize Snackley's revolver. He pressed it against Snackley's side.

The smuggler gave in. He flung his arms above his head.

"I'm licked," he muttered sullenly.

They got slowly to their feet, Fenton Hardy keeping a watchful eye on the captive. Upstairs they could hear the uproar continuing as the police still gave battle to the smugglers.

"Upstairs!" snapped the detective curtly. Without taking his eyes off Snackley he said to the man on the cot.

"We'll come back for you later—Mr. Jones."

CHAPTER XXIV

THE ROUND-UP

The Hardy boys, in the meantime, were in the thick of the struggle.

Frank fought desperately with the smuggler he had assailed in the living room of the house, while Joe raced across the yard toward the trapdoor leading to the underground caves. He found that although three of the smugglers had been captured by officers in the yard and that as many more were fighting to escape, none of the police had as yet learned of the trapdoor down which some of the men had disappeared.

With a shout to a near-by officer who had just succeeded in clapping the handcuffs on one of the smugglers, Joe made his way down the stairs. He heard the officer running over to the edge of the trap and saw the gleam of the flashlight.

"Some of them got out this way!" Joe shouted back to the officer.

The man called to one of his companions and then footsteps clattered on the stairs as Joe went on.

He reached the door that opened into the chamber where his father had been a prisoner, but on entering the room he found it empty. There were evidences of hasty flight and the door on the far side of the room was wide open.

"Secret passages, eh!" exclaimed one of the officers, as he came into the room. He was a state trooper in uniform.

Joe led the way out through the opposite door and down the stairs that led toward the bottom of the cliff. The trooper who had spoken illuminated the way with his flashlight and they clattered on down the stairs until they reached the storage room. Here, everything was in confusion. The escaping smugglers had evidently endeavored to take with them what goods they could, probably the smaller packages containing drugs, for boxes and parcels were overturned and strewn about the floor.

"You seem to know this place pretty well," said one of the troopers, as Joe led the way across to the opposite door and stepped out onto the landing.

"I've been here before—got in this way," he answered. "There's a water cave below this passage. They've probably made their getaway in the boat."

They hastened down the passageway and came at last to the cave. As Joe expected, the boat was gone.

"They got away," he said, in disappointment, as the trooper turned the flashlight on to the channel between the rocks.

There was a shout from the darkness of the cove.

"Give us a light!" they heard.

Joe gave a shout of joy. It was Tony Prito's voice!

Then Joe and the troopers with him heard the steady beat of a motorboat.

Joe seized the flashlight and ran out along the path leading to the entrance of the cave.

The motorboat was not many yards away. Tony had been searching for the channel.

"Right this way!" Joe called out. "Head toward the right of the cave and you'll be in deep water. A little further! Good!"

As the motorboat drew nearer he saw that it was filled with men and that a rowboat was being towed behind.

"We got 'em," cried Tony exultantly. "They were just getting out of the cove in the boat when we came up."

"Who is with you?" asked Joe.

"Police. The rest of them went up the shore road in a car."

"We've caught the whole gang then. They raided the house and got rest of the smugglers. We thought these fellows had made a getaway."

"No chance. Although it was mighty close. They pretty nearly slipped out of the cove right under our noses."

The boat came to a stop beside the natural wharf of rock. One or two of the officers, revolvers in hand, clambered out. Three of the smugglers had been captured while trying to escape from the cove in the rowboat.

"If they'd got out we would never have caught them," said Joe. "They were heading out toward a ship."

"A ship!" exclaimed one of the officers, a burly man in plain clothes. He stepped forward. "Did they say anything about a ship?"

"A man named Li Chang has a ship lying in wait outside the bay," said Joe. "I heard them talking about it."

"Good!" exclaimed the burly man. "Now we'll capture the whole outfit." He turned to Tony. "I suppose your boat is good for another little run."

"I'll say it is, sir!"

"I want as many officers as we can spare," said the burly man. "We'll go out and find that ship. Li Chang, did you say?" he added, turning to Joe.

"That was the name."

"I know his ship. We've been trying to catch that villain for years. Darst, go on up and see how the rest of the men made out at the house on the cliff and take as many officers as they can spare. There's a passage up through the rocks, I take it?"

"Regular staircase all the way, sir," remarked Darst, one of the raiding officers.

"Good! Don't lose any time."

The three smugglers were taken out of the boat and handcuffed, then escorted up the stairs, while the burly man, who was the chief of a squad of federal agents undertaking a drive against the smugglers on that part of the coast, remained with the motorboat.

Within a short time Darst returned with three more officers. He reported that a clean sweep had been made at the house.

"They have 'em all handcuffed and sittin' in the kitchen," he said. "Mr. Hardy got Snackley—"

"Snackley?" exclaimed the federal man. "Is it *his* gang?"

"Yes, sir. He got Snackley in the cellar. One of his sons tackled Redhead Blount, one of Snackley's sidekicks, and held him down until the police came in. When we brought our three in, that finished the round-up."

"It does, so far. We're going out and grab Li Chang from that ship and that'll clean everything up."

The officers got into the motorboat and Joe clambered in beside Tony Prito, who was at the wheel. The craft backed out of the channel into the deeper water of the cove, then sped out into Barmet Bay.

"Once we get out of the bay we should see her lights," said the federal officer. "Li Chang probably has his ship anchored just off the coast."

This proved to be the case. The lights of the vessel were soon descried and the motorboat sped toward it through the night.

When the boat drew alongside, the federal man roared out:

"Ahoy, there!"

A voice answered in Chinese.

"Speak English!" roared the officer. "Throw over a ladder or we'll open fire on you."

"Who there?"

"The police."

Jabbering voices and running footsteps suddenly created a commotion. One of the troopers fired his revolver into the air and very promptly a ladder was lowered over the side of the vessel.

"That's better!" said the federal man, as he clambered up over the rail, revolver in hand. "I'll just talk to your skipper for a minute."

The capture of Li Chang was without incident. When he was told that Snackley and the gang were captured, the Chinaman, who was a small, wizened little fellow with a villainous countenance, blandly submitted to arrest and consented to be taken ashore. There were only two or three members of the crew aboard, the others having shore leave; so two of the federal men were left in charge of the ship until relief could be sent from Bayport, and the motorboat made its way back to the cove.

The round-up was complete. Snackley's smuggling gang had been completely broken up.

CHAPTER XXV

THE MYSTERY EXPLAINED

The Hardy boys were the heroes of Bayport when the news of the capture of Snackley and his men spread throughout the city next day. As for Tony Prito, he was the envy of all the chums of the two lads.

"Tony had all the luck," bemoaned Chet Morton, as the boys were all sitting in the barn back of the Hardy home next afternoon. This barn, which had been fitted up as a gymnasium, was a meeting place for the lads on occasions of importance.

"We had to have a motorboat," said Frank. "Believe me, I was wishing more than once that the whole crowd was along."

"And you'll get the reward for capturing Snackley?" asked Phil Cohen.

"Not all of it. Dad gets half. Joe and I split the rest."

"You haven't any kick coming. What's going to happen to Snackley?"

"He'll probably go to the electric chair," answered Frank soberly.

"Why?"

"He murdered Felix Polucca, the miser."

"Murdered him?"

"Yes. Dad found that out in his investigations. Dad suspected all along that there was some connection between Snackley and the house on the cliff, especially when he found that Snackley and Polucca had been related. He went out to find out what he could, but the smugglers saw him and captured him."

"What about that fellow they had imprisoned in the cellar?" questioned Biff Hooper. "Didn't you say Snackley was just going to kill him when your father saved him?"

"That was the young fellow we saved in the bay that day. The young chap who told us his name was Jones. It wasn't his real name, at all. His name is Yates and he was one of the smugglers."

"Why was Snackley chasing him that day?" asked Perry Robinson.

"It seems that Yates got angry because he didn't get his full share of the money from the last smuggling trip, so he threatened to tell the police on Snackley. The smugglers locked him up, but he got away in one of the motorboats, so they chased him and ran him down. They thought to have killed him in the explosion or else drown him, but Joe and I managed to bring him ashore. We left him at the Kane farmhouse, but the smugglers came along next day and kidnapped him. They kept him prisoner in the cellar of the Polucca place after that."

"I still can't understand about those yells and shrieks we heard the first day we were out at the farmhouse," put in Phil Cohen.

"That was just to frighten us away. One of the men in the gang is a sort of half-wit and they had him posted there to frighten people off by yelling and shrieking whenever any one showed up around the place. He was the chap who stole our tools from the motorcycles," explained Frank.

"But after our visit there," added Joe, "they thought it was too dangerous and that there might be an investigation, so they put Redhead and his wife and one of their men there to pose as renters of the place."

"So there weren't any ghosts after all," exclaimed Jerry Gilroy.

"Nary a ghost," laughed Frank, "Snackley explained everything this morning in a confession. The whole gang is locked up, even to Li Chang. Yates, the young fellow they had kept prisoner so long, told the whole story first. He turned state's evidence and told how long the smuggling had been going on, how Snackley had made use of the house on the cliff after killing Polucca, how he fixed up the tunnels in the cliff—he told everything. It seems that Polucca had the smuggling idea in the first place and he spent years fixing up those caves and tunnels. When everything was ready, he called in Snackley, but Snackley didn't like to share with any one who had a right to a voice in the affair, so he killed the old man, took his money, and brought the smuggling gang in there."

"Yates told all that?"

"He told so much of it that Snackley saw there was no use bluffing any longer, so he admitted the whole story."

"Gosh!" sighed Chet. "Just my luck! I was there in time to get scared to death by that half-wit, and there in time to get bawled out and chased off the farm by Redhead and his wife, but I missed out on all the fun at the last."

"Not much fun about it," declared Joe. "It didn't seem funny to us when the smugglers caught us in the cave just as we were getting dad free."

"And it wasn't any fun hiding in that attic with the bullets coming through the floor, nineteen to the dozen," added Frank. "I thought every minute was going to be my last."

"No, I guess it wasn't any too funny then," admitted Chet. "You deserve every cent you get out of the reward."

"We'll treat the whole gang to a feed as soon as we collect," Joe promised.

"Whee!" shouted Chet, turning a handspring. "Now you're talking!"

The Hardy boys kept their word. Soon after they had received their share of the reward, which was presented to them with many glowing words and congratulations from the federal authorities who had long been trying to put Snackley behind the bars, they gave a dinner in the barn that eclipsed any similar "feed" in the history of Bayport.

"I hope the Hardy boys solve a mystery every week," said Chet, as he confronted his third dish of ice-cream. "And I hope they celebrate every success the same way."

The Hardy boys were not destined to solve a mystery every week, but it was not long before they were plunged into a maze of events which were fully as exciting as those which led to the finding of the tower treasure and those that followed their first visit to the house on the cliff. The story of their adventures will be told in the next volume of this series, called, "The Hardy Boys: The Secret of the Old Mill."

Tony Prito, conscious of the envying glances of the other lads because he had participated in the eventful climax to the mystery of the house on the cliff, scooped up the last of his ice-cream and said:

"Once I wanted my father to buy an automobile and he bought a motorboat instead. Now he wants to sell the boat and buy an automobile. Just let him try it! That boat gave me more fun in one day than I'd ever had since we came to the States."

THE END

Made in the USA
Monee, IL
26 October 2024